Jer. 29:11
Enjoy!
"Elle"

SEBEWAING LIBRARY
41 North Center
Sebewaing, MI 48759

Miracle in the City of Angels

An International Adoption Story

by

Elle Conner
and
Erin Brown Conroy, MA

AuthorHouse™
1663 Liberty Drive, Suite 200
Bloomington, IN 47403
www.authorhouse.com
Phone: 1-800-839-8640

© 2007 Elle Conner and Erin Brown Conroy, MA. All rights reserved.

No part of this book may be reproduced, stored in a retrieval system, or transmitted by any means without the written permission of the author.

First published by AuthorHouse 8/27/2007

ISBN: 978-1-4343-3367-4 (sc)

Printed in the United States of America
Bloomington, Indiana

This book is printed on acid-free paper.

authorHOUSE®

Dedications

To my immediate family: I love you with all of my heart and I thank God every day for each one of you.

Mom, you have been invaluable. None of this would have happened without your guidance, support, and love. Thank you.

To our extended family: Thank you for all the hands-on help with raising our children. You are appreciated and loved.

Erin: Your writing style has turned "Miracle" into the story it is today. Thank you for your expertise.

Praise for
Miracle in the City of Angels

"As a German-born adoptee, I found *Miracle in the City of Angels* tugged at my heart. The luscious emotion-filled descriptions brought me to each page fully present and carried me from one page to another voraciously. It's a must-read that brings real, heartfelt perspective for all whose lives are touched by adoption." - Lissa Ann Forbes, author of *Write from the Inside: Dig for Treasures, Discover Yourself, Leave a Legacy*

"Miracle in the City of Angels answers the most pressing questions hopeful adoptive parents have – what is it really like and how will I feel? Conner and Conroy bring the reader along on the adoption journey and provide amazing insight into the ups, downs, and tangents the adoption journey is made up of. This is the most honest and real adoption narrative you will ever encounter and I recommend it to every person considering adoption. It is a joy to read." - Brette Sember, author of *The Adoption Answer Book*

2006

Introduction

From Elle

In a rush, the endless suspended feeling of waiting fell forward – culminating, cascading into one sweet, precious moment – a moment beyond words. Beyond feeling. Beyond anything I could have whispered in my thoughts or penned in my Journal.

It's the moment I first saw my baby daughter face-to-face.

This book is a story of international adoption, chronicling thousands of footsteps on the journey to my daughter. The adoption process is an expedition that pulls you, draws you, presses at you, and ultimately completes you. From the first cautious moments of your decision to adopt – to the overwhelming moment of greeting your son or daughter for the very first time – those pursuing international adoption walk a passage filled with wonderings, longings, and questions.

"What is it really like? What's ahead for me – as I work through all the details, the paperwork, the home visits, the phone calls, and all of the other 'hoops to jump through'? Will the squeezing, pressing waiting ever end? Will I ever get to those breathtaking seconds of seeing, touching, and holding my child for the very first time? Who can truly understand what I'm feeling? Are the feelings that I have right now 'normal'?"

From Erin

Just like Elle, my husband and I have faced those same questions – five separate times, for eight children, all born overseas and brought into our family as precious sons and daughters. For all adoptive parents, these questions nudge us. Sometimes they poke at us in a bothersome kind of way. And sometimes they grab us and roar in our ears, interjecting from the shadows of the day and keeping us from sleep at night.

Our questions are natural, normal. They're expected. And they beg for answers.

This story gives you answers.

From the Both of Us

If you're walking the journey right now, waiting for your child to come home, then this book is for you. Read these pages and know that you're not alone. Learn the scenery of the journey. Feel peace that what you're experiencing is "OK." And, perhaps most importantly, feel the hope that the journey *does* eventually end. You *do* get to the destination – joyfully receiving your child.

If you know someone in the process of international adoption, and you want to walk alongside in empathy, then this book is for you too. Understand what the waiting adoptive parent experiences and feels. Through new understanding, be a better mom or dad, sister or brother, aunt or uncle, co-worker and friend.

If you're contemplating the journey of international adoption, then this book is a candid look at how it all works. Throughout the story, these pages answer the most common questions of international adoption. You'll gain a clearer picture of the whole process. You'll dare to dream. Our hope is that you'll be inspired and encouraged to make the journey – to give a waiting child a hope-filled future.

If you're an adoptee, this book adds layers of understanding to the *whys* and *hows* of what your mom and dad went through to bring you home. In these pages, you find empathy, perception, and awareness – bringing the power to pencil in a more complete picture of who you are. By giving dimension to the understanding of how deeply you were desired, fought for, and cherished *right from the start*, we pray that you will feel and believe in your indescribable value.

From Elle
This is my story; but, in some ways, it's your story too. Come.
> Walk with me.
> Laugh and cry with me.
> Adoptive moms and dads, find out what's ahead.
> Family and friends, come alongside.
> Curious observers, explore the possibilities.
> Sons and daughters, find another piece of who you are.

From Erin
This book is the first of three. To protect the anonymity of the family in sequel books, the names of the author ("Elle" in this story) and her relatives and friends have been changed. The people and events are real.

As you place one foot in front of the other on the international adoption path, know that the end is worth all of the work and struggle to get there. The moments of waiting fall into one: The powerful uniting of parent and child.

Come. Let's walk together.

Contents

Introduction	vii
Chapter One In the Beginning	1
Chapter Two Our Family	7
Chapter Three The Time is Right	13
Chapter Four The Home Study	19
Chapter Five Paperwork, Paperwork	23
Chapter Six Personal Connection	29
Chapter Seven The Real Waiting Begins	35
Chapter Eight Ups and Downs	41
Chapter Nine Wait Upon the Lord	47
Chapter Ten The Video	51
Chapter Eleven Our Little Girl	55
Chapter Twelve Medical Fears	59

Chapter Thirteen 　Truly Ours	65
Chapter Fourteen 　In Angels' Arms	71
Chapter Fifteen 　The Phone Call	77
Chapter Sixteen 　Preparing to Leave	83
Chapter Seventeen 　A Mother's Heart	87
Chapter Eighteen 　Over the Ocean	93
Chapter Nineteen 　Welcome in St. Petersburg	99
Chapter Twenty 　Exploring with Zibi	105
Chapter Twenty-One 　The Royal City	111
Chapter Twenty-Two 　Into the City of Angels	115
Chapter Twenty-Three 　Hello, My Little One	121
Chapter Twenty-Four 　Settling In	127
Chapter Twenty-Five 　The Meal	133
Chapter Twenty-Six 　Forward Steps	141
Chapter Twenty-Seven 　The Proceedings Begin	149

Chapter Twenty-Eight
    Courtroom Intensity   155

Chapter Twenty-Nine
    The Baby Room   161

Chapter Thirty
    Baptism with our Russian Five   165

Chapter Thirty-One
    Goodbye to the City of Angels   171

Chapter Thirty-Two
    Moscow   177

Chapter Thirty-Three
    The Last Leg   183

Chapter Thirty-Four
    Home   189

Chapter One

In the Beginning

I have to admit, when I first saw the Journal, it didn't strike me as anything special. But I knew it was "the right one." Flipping through the bin at the dollar store, its cover's creamy caramel color stood out, leaning quietly against the gaudy bright pink journals designed for teen girls. Its simplicity drew me in. Pulling the blank book from the bin, my fingers ran along its smooth cloth. I placed the Journal in the empty plastic basket hanging from the crook of my arm.

This will do.

In that simple moment, I had no idea. I had no idea of the future significance of this plain, inexpensive book. Like a seamstress first placing a needle in cloth, to create an intricate garment, the prick of this point in time pierced the fabric of my life. I needed this Journal for a specific reason: Today, Jonathan and I decided to begin the process to adopt a child from overseas. And in an impulsive and compelling kind of way, buying the Journal seemed like the right thing to do.

Jonathan and I talked about adoption before. In fact, it was before Michael and Thomas were born, before we were married, and before we'd even finished college together.

I met Jonathan in 1985, at the start of my sophomore year at Ferris State. I escaped an abusive relationship only months earlier, and to tell you the truth, it felt good to be back at school. I wanted life to be normal, maybe even boring. School seemed like the perfect way to get into the mundane. Love was the least of my priorities. But then along came Jonathan. Or, should I say, in jumped Jonathan.

It was right after German language class. My new friend and dorm-mate Naomi and I were walking down the corridor together. We'd only just met yesterday. You know how it is when you first meet someone: The both of you are cautious, asking questions, a bit on edge. So here we were walking down the hall, my tall legs matching Naomi's stride, her brown hair swinging in time with my long blonde hair, chatting about who-knows-what.

Then, mid-sentence, right out of the shadows with a whoop and holler, a guy grabbed Naomi and, like a wildcat, jumped onto her back. My heart jumped wildly; immediately my thoughts raced to the day-before's campus safety lecture. Whirling in panic, a burst of Naomi's infectious laughter echoed through the hallway.

What in the world...?! Mouth open, blinking, I breathed again.

Noticing my pale face, Naomi pulled away from the guy's gangly, grabbing limbs to reach out and put her hand on my arm. "Are you OK?" I smiled weakly and nodded once. *As OK as I could be, with my palms sweating, heart thumping, and mind racing from the adrenaline rush.*

With a look of apology, Naomi said, "Elle, this is my brother, Jonathan." "Oh. Hi." I tried to smile, but I'm sure it came out polite and stiff. It was going to take a while for my tight chest to get back to normal. *What kind of guy jumps on people like that?*

I have to admit, it took more than a few days to get over my first impression of Jonathan. I went back to my dorm room that day thinking he must be absolutely crazy. Handsome, but crazy.

But as the days of fall semester passed, I realized there was much more to this guy. Because of Naomi, the three of us spent a lot of time together. He really was shy (something that took me a while to believe, after our first meeting), and for the most part, quiet in crowds, reserved, and polite. A level thinker. And oh yes, calm. In those first months, I gained a sense of Jonathan's quiet and gentle nature, a deep river running in and through his life with purpose, strength, and faith. Very different from my first impression.

I'm not exactly sure when it was, but there came a moment when I perceived something stronger between us. Maybe that "something stronger" sprouted when sitting on the grungy brown shag carpet in his apartment, listening together to the latest Alabama album. Maybe it grew during those hours when we sipped sweet bubbles from bottles of pop, talked, and laughed about his growing up as one of twelve children. Well, I know for sure that later on, on that cool spring night of '86, we both sensed a change; delicate roots of a future together had quietly woven down into the earth of both our lives.

That particular spring night, we studied for a couple of hours in "the dungeon," the dark room in the basement of Vandercook Dorm named for obvious reasons. My head hurt from the thickness of the room, making it hard to concentrate. Feeling a bit claustrophobic, thoughts kept sneaking out to wonder about the fresh spring air. I placed my book aside, sighed, and stretched. *I really need to get out of here.*

"Jonathan, can we take a break and take a walk or something?"

"Sure," he answered. "But let's finish this problem first." Jonathan's matter-of-fact, stick-to-it-ive-ness showed even then.

With the sun down, the cool evening air tickled the skin on my arms. It felt really good. Jonathan slipped his hand into mine, and a warm blanket of peace draped itself around my shoulders.

We meandered toward the river; this was our place of privacy. The water murmured over rocks, and from the corner of my eye, a slight movement made me turn. In silence, a bat swooped down to the face of the river; danced to snatch a bug, and then disappeared. Neither one of us spoke. Intuitively, we let our fingers slip apart and sat on the bank, close, almost touching but not, looking over the water. Early evening sounds fell in a gentle backdrop around us.

"Jonathan?"

"Hmmm?" The sound of his voice told me he listened intently.

"I know family's really important to you." As I spoke, his eyes moved from the river to my face. He turned and leaned down on one elbow. I continued.

"How many children do you hope to have someday?"

Jonathan answered right away. "Oh, two or three."

We both fell quiet again, thinking. A full minute passed while the river continued in soft conversation in front of us. Then I spoke again.

"You know I've had medical problems....We talked about it before. I mean, you know – medical problems that might not allow me to have children." I realized the last words bunched together just a little bit as they came out. He didn't answer.

I paused, feeling the silence. It wasn't a bad silence. So I went on.

"And I also know that family's really important to you."

His gaze didn't move; he looked directly, with a safe kindness, the river reflecting in his eyes. His jet-black wiry hair lay close to his head, the well-trimmed cut barely moving in the breeze. For some reason, the muscles in my arms felt a little tight, almost achy. I shifted, rubbed one arm, and looked at the ground. Reaching, I tugged on a long piece of grass. The soft spring shoot came into my hand with ease.

Rolling the sliver of green between my fingers, I turned.

"Even if by some miracle I have biological children, I'd like to adopt one day."

He and I both knew my words weren't broad brush strokes about the general future; we were talking about *our* future.

"That's cool." His words were quiet and measured. My body relaxed a bit. "Didn't you tell me your best friend in high school was adopted as a baby?"

I nodded, a smile warming across my face, remembering moments giggling together like sisters. Yes, that friendship showed me the impact of an adoptive family's love on a single life.

Squinting his eyes a bit, Jonathan looked across the river, his gaze far beyond the physical boundaries of earth and water. Then he nodded and spoke again. "There are a lot of babies born that need good moms and dads. Maybe we can adopt someday."

It was a pronouncement. Not a wishful, wispy kind of statement. Then he turned back. "God will let us know when and if He wants that for us."

I marveled at his faith. It emanated from him in a plain, firm way. That kind of faith was new, intriguing. My mom and dad took me to church as a little girl, but when my dad's cancer weakened him, we stopped going. Later, after dad died, mom and I returned only for Christmas and Easter. Church held strange, cold shadows of death mixed with life. It was distant.

This kind of faith felt different. This faith – this deep sense of abiding in truth – was like a beautiful wooden ship with masts, sailing tall and proud, able to anchor firm when winds whipped and the sea screamed in anger.

"Elle." He spoke my name quietly and firmly. "Will you attend confirmation classes to become Lutheran? It's important to me. I want my future wife to go to church with me." The weight of his words moved in a wave through my whole body, leaving my heart's rhythm pressing strong against my chest. I didn't want to breathe.

He leaned in, face close to mine.

"And it will make it easier for us when we raise our family."

He said, "Our family."

My answer came simple and sure. "Yes."

Yes to this faith.
Yes to the rest of my life with you.
And yes to our future adopted child.

Chapter Two

Our Family

Weekends turned into travels home to meet Jonathan's family in Michigan. The first time we drove, Jonathan and I talked the whole way. That's when I found out about July 7, 1976. That's the date Jonathan's mother died. Jonathan was ten years old. It was a heart attack, right there in the front of the house, while she worked in the garden. Her death left Grandpa Casey alone with eleven kids. Can you imagine? I'm surprised he waited the three years he did, to marry Claire.

I liked Jonathan's dad and Claire right away; from that first "hello," the warmth for their son spilled around me. Jonathan's two brothers and their families, who lived within a few miles of his mom and dad, received me in the same kindness. It was as if I stepped into the stream of their lives and swirled around the family's every-day movements, like a leaf swept away on the top of a dancing current.

Life there was so "typical small town." Everyone knew everyone. In a few short months, it seemed like I visited every family, ate just about every kind of meat-and-potato meal, and sat around just about every size and shape of kitchen table ever made.

I remember arriving for one particular meal at Jonathan's brother and wife's home. When we rang the bell and the door opened, the smell of crock pot dinner that had been simmering all afternoon poured out and around us. It was the kind of rich smell that permeates and sinks into your clothes in a good kind of way.

We stepped from the cool dark outside into warm yellow lampshade light. Hellos bubbled around us. When I walked into the kitchen and dining room, I noticed the darkness pressing up against the window panes like a black wall. Standing inside, safety surrounded us and firmly held the blackness out.

After dinner, perched on bar stools at the high counter, we nibbled rock candy and talked. Sometimes I just watched and listened. Thinking back now, one word comes to mind: blessed. Life in that small town felt blessed. And I felt so blessed, to be a part of it.

I think the family's faith had a lot to do with how they accepted me. Jonathan's family prayed before every single meal. I have to admit, that was something new. But then – get this – after the meal, they passed the Bible around, and different members of the family read that particular night's "devotion." I sat there, listening, curious, a little uncomfortable at first. But it felt so right.

On Sunday mornings, we all packed into the car and drove to the small church in town. On one of those Sundays not too long after that evening at the river with Jonathan, I asked the pastor if I could join their special class to become a member. The pastor's face got a look that I won't forget – with a smile and nod I imagine St. Nick might have while placing an anticipated gift under the tree. Now I knew what it meant to have a "church family." It felt good.

I had a million questions about God. There was so much about this faith thing that I didn't understand…and I wanted to know it all, *right now*. Of course, that didn't happen. Sometimes we have to wait, like the feeling of being in a long line where you don't see the end, and you don't even know what's at the end – but it has to be good. I now understood that sometimes we don't get the answers we're looking for. And maybe sometimes we don't get answers at all. I started to grasp the fact that that's part of the definition of "faith." I guess I realized early on that I need to let God be God.

That's so hard.

I don't know where the rest of those college years went. We became a "couple," living a rhythm of classes, visiting home, and getting to know each other. Each summer, Jonathan lived with his parents while working at the local tool and engineering company. I went to my hometown in southwest Michigan for half the summer, and then for the second half, lived with my grandparents in Ohio. I'm sure my grandparents grew sick of me talking about Jonathan. Grandpa took advantage of the moment and countered my chatter with old-fashioned advice on love.

I listened.

Aside from summers, Jonathan and I "grew up" together in those years. Sure, we had our ups and downs. But we never grew apart. We were on the path of a future together, and we knew it.

In March of 1989, Jonathan and I were married. We promptly moved into a small rental house just a few miles from his parents and brothers. Yes, I stepped into small town life with grace and eagerness – while Jonathan stepped into a full-time job at the same tool and engineering company.

I took the wife role seriously. After experiencing all of the wonderful meals with Jonathan's family, I felt horrible at my disastrous attempts at cooking. I first "mastered" the roast-potato-carrot dinner; we ate it an awful lot. Jonathan never complained once. That's so Jonathan.

When it came to friends, the first years were tough. I met Jonathan's former high school classmates; they all had so much in common, and I was the outsider. The only one I really "clicked with" was Sarah. Already a mom of a toddler, Sarah seemed so much wiser and experienced in just about everything in life. Sarah was sweet and talkative, and with her black hair and smooth white skin, she reminded me of Snow White.

I liked having a friend like Snow White.

One day, Jonathan and I purchased three acres of wooded land at the edge of town. What a glorious day! Even though it would be years before building on the lot, it was so fun to spend time there clearing debris and making plans to build our dream house. Even when we bought our two-story Tasha Tudor home on Center Street in town, we dreamed of our future family – in a home, on that land.

Life was so good.

But then one day, I physically didn't feel well. My stomach bothered me. I mean *really* bothered me. And the sick ache didn't get better with time; it grew. For days in a row, morning to night, nausea rolled around my body in undulating waves. Since his job seemed to be extra-stressful lately, I didn't want to bother Jonathan with it. But I was worried.

I decided to call Sarah.

"Sarah?" Sarah always answered on the first ring.

"Hi Elle!" And it never failed: The tone in her voice was like I was the one person on the face of the earth that she really wanted to talk to, and that she was so glad that I called.

"Hey, do you have a moment?" She did, of course. I told her how awful I felt over the last week or so.

"Oh, come on! Don't you get it?" Sarah quipped.

"Get that I'm sick?" On the other end of the line, Sarah laughed at my naiveté. The bubbly laughter triggered a tiny thought that started at my neck in a flush, then rushed through my body with a tingle of realization.

"Are you trying to say that I might be pregnant?"

"Of course!"

I gasped. Then giggled. Then nervously pronounced, "Sarah, come on! I don't believe you!"

"Elle, do me a favor. Go to the doctor for a quick test. For goodness sakes, you only live a mile away from the office!"

At that moment, I was glad for small town living and the fact that everything was "a hop, skip, and a jump away."

Within five minutes I sat in the doctor's small exam room. The nurse came into the room with a big smile and broadcast, "Positive!"

My head spun in dizzy delight. With joy bursting from every part of me, I grabbed my jacket. Jonathan was due home from work any minute. I *had* to be there when he got home.

And I was. As soon as I flung my jacket on the chair, the back door thumped closed. My words tumbled out before Jonathan even rounded the hallway corner.

"I haven't felt well, and I was nauseous, and I talked to Sarah, and she said to go, and I did, and they did a test, and it was positive!" Though Jonathan had no idea what I was talking about, he immediately caught the joy in my voice and flash in my eyes.

"W-wait a minute! What did you say?"

"Yes, we're going to have a baby!"

Everything was so perfect. We told a few people right away and the whole town knew. We held hands a lot, and congratulations flew around our ears while at the grocery store and while walking down the street. I loved waking up.

Then the perfect world fell apart.

I miscarried the baby.

I didn't know pain existed like this. I'd always heard phrases for pain like, "My heart felt ripped out of my chest." Well it's true. But the awful ripping doesn't happen just once. It keeps going. The horrifying burning and throbbing in your soul happens again and again. Over time, I found the pain and loss wasn't quite as intense as in the beginning. Its keen and powerful grip of dreadfulness rounded off to become numb around the edges.

But then it ached.

My days felt broken. Jonathan didn't say it, but I saw the shattered feeling in his eyes. My thoughts randomly wandered, sifting through the glass shards of raw emotion and loss. I needed something to sweep it all away. Or, at the very least, I needed something to stare at, to bring a feeling of hope. I focused my mind on the fact that I was able to conceive.

Falling asleep at night was more than difficult; it was awful. I dreaded sleep because I'd wake up in the middle of the night from dreams where I couldn't find my baby. Throwing the comforter around, patting the mattress, frantically searching – it took minutes for Jonathan to wake me from the nightmares. When I fully awoke, and reality hit me hard again, Jonathan held me while I swayed in grief and cried.

Weeks passed. The haunting memory of the D & C clung to me day and night.

Then one morning, the nausea returned. This time, I knew what it was, and I welcomed the queasiness with relief.

Jonathan's blue eyes sparkled as he gazed into my soul and spoke words of melodic hope: "This time, it will be different."

I clung to his declaration.

And every morning, I clung to the toilet, vomiting, crying, and flushing. I don't know how he did it, but Jonathan looked past it all.

"You look beautiful this morning. You're glowing."

A ragged smile graced my face. "Are you sure the 'radiant glow' isn't the reflection of the toilet water?"

Along with clinging to the toilet, I clung to new-found humor – anything to help me get through this constant throwing-up routine. And in that routine, like whispering a secret to myself over and over, I clung desperately to the intense desire for this baby to be alright.

Our marriage roots grew deeper. The emotional rebound from the miscarriage's pain flung me into this second-joy with a passion that brought us incredibly close. When we snuggled on the couch, I placed Jonathan's hand on my abdomen. We held our breath in those miraculous moments when the baby moved. A protruding elbow or knee rolled under his touch and then disappeared to make my taut melon-belly round again.

I took nothing for granted.

Jonathan is a brilliant gift from God. I never thought I'd have a second brilliant gift, but it came. On February 3, 1992, God gave me Michael.

Michael became my whole world. Everything – I mean *everything* – revolved around feeding time, nap time, diaper time, and play time. Deliriously happy, I spent hours looking at his tiny nose, itsy eyelashes, and delicate fingers. Jonathan often came home on lunch break to find me sitting in the big reclining chair, baby in arms, gazing into Michael's big brown eyes. The same eyes as my father.

My world, now a trio of mom-dad-baby busy-ness, brought bounty and beauty into the mundane. It was probably the world and experience of every new mom and dad, but for me, it was healing. It was life increasing in joy.

This kind of joy made me thirsty. Thirsty for more.

Jonathan and I both knew our world was not complete. Our family was only beginning.

Chapter Three

The Time is Right

After Michael's birth, it didn't take long for me to get pregnant again. It wasn't hard to tell, because my old friend Nausea returned with a fury. And he never left. He marched right in and made himself at home, sitting right in the middle of my living room with his muddy feet up on my coffee table. With cheeky irreverence, he followed me from room to room and place to place. It didn't matter if it was morning, mid-afternoon, or the middle of the night; waves lurched in my stomach. I felt as if Nausea moved me out of my home and threw me onto a flimsy dingy, repeatedly flung high and low in the middle of the Atlantic.

From the beginning of this pregnancy, all was not well. The doctor's worry sent me to the hospital for ultrasounds. Over and over, I dragged my tired body in to that four-walled infirmary. There were the IV drips. And multiple doses of drugs to stop the labor pangs that wouldn't stop. Looking into my little Michael's face and imagining the new little one to come, I knew this physical misery was going to be worth it all. But after nine months, my tired body hung disheveled and worn. My mom came to live with us. She stayed by my side much of the time. I felt like a little girl.

Then news came: Grandma suffered a brain aneurism and lay in the hospital. Mom left that day, knowing the purpose of her hello to her own mom was really to say goodbye.

Grandma stayed alive long enough to whisper "I love you's" to her daughters – my mom and her sister – before she died.

I never had the chance to say goodbye.

Alone, physically exhausted, and feeling vulnerable, memories of moments with Grandma floated in and out of my mind, teasing, tormenting. On the day of the funeral, Jonathan was at work; I lay pressed into the light-blue floral couch in my living room and sobbed. My tears flowed into dark, wet splotches on the printed cloth petals.

Michael toddled up to the edge of the couch. At almost two years of age, he knew something dreadful made my body tremble. Tenuously, he brought his favorite puppy book and pressed it to my chest. Then he placed his little arm over my big belly. I looked intently into his pure eyes. His fingers traced my abdomen, a sizeable mound next to his small frame.

"Hi baby." Those two sweet words pushed away the pain and brought me to the precious present. Jonathan came home to find us asleep there, together, on the couch, the puppy book tucked between us.

The next day, Sarah drove me to my scheduled doctor appointment.

"Elle." The doctor's tone of voice made my eyes flit to Sarah's face.

"You need to go directly to the hospital. Right now."

Sarah's arms started scooping up my things, and the doctor at once took my arm and helped lower my bulk to the floor.

"You're going to have that baby *today*."

His verdict pressed into my eardrums, sending strong pulses of excited energy into my body that made my hands sweat. I don't remember the car ride there; I do remember what felt like Sarah tucking me in to the bed in the hospital room. And I remember her picking up the pale plastic phone next to the bed and calling Jonathan.

The nurse scurried in, hooking up tubes and wires. Sarah kept scooting to the left, then to the right, shifting from foot to foot and trying to straighten the wrinkles on the bed sheets. Then she spoke, words sounding pencil thin. "Please don't do anything to speed up the labor." Sarah's eyes looked to me, then to the nurse, then to the door, then back to me.

"Please wait until the father arrives."

I wanted Jonathan there too.

Jonathan arrived breathless. Splashes of those first excited moments stretched into numbing hours of pain, with only little drop-like moments of relief: ice chips on my tongue, Jonathan's awkward finger tips pensively spreading creamy lip balm on my lips, gentle touches of assurance on my back. Like a Dali painting, the surreal sounds of "Jeopardy" from the hanging television droned on, mixing with antiseptic smells and rustlings of the intrusive comings and goings of hospital staff.

Sensations blurred time with pain. Jonathan's face there, then not. The nurse. No, nurses. A midwife. More movement beside the bed, touching my side. Pain swallowing me. Movement through and down. A small baby's cry. Much movement. Jonathan near my ear, whispering, "Thomas is here." Pressing, afterbirth. Where is my son? There. Right there. Nurses are huddled around, arms moving quickly. Doing what? I can't see. The midwife turned her face upwards to me and spoke.

"This baby is a miracle. The placenta is tangled and torn. He shouldn't be alive. But he's perfect." They brought Thomas to me, wrapped in blankets, and laid him in the cradle of my arm. My universe throbbed in joy against lingering physical pain.

There, in the center of Thomas's forehead, lay a faint red mark.

Jonathan squinted his eyes and gently reached out to touch the mark with the tip of his index finger. Thomas ever-so-slightly moved under his touch.

"What is it?" he asked the nurse.

Before the nurse could answer, my faint voice interrupted.

"It's a kiss. . . " I paused, voice hanging. Jonathan's eyes met mine. "…a kiss, from Grandma."

A child kissed from heaven. A miracle.

My third brilliant gift from God.

Life has a way of making miracles fade. But the miracle of my two boys never dulled. In vivid color, I saw my father's smile juxtaposed over Michael's grin. In layers of melody, I heard my grandmother's laugh melodically join in over Thomas's giggles. In pulsing dances, I felt the breeze on my skin while watching my sons play on the grass – the same dancing breeze from the river, when Jonathan and I first imagined our children.

My hand stretched out to Life, and Life placed moment after moment of gem stones into my palm. I knew I'd never have another child by birth; the doctor informed us, warned us: "Too dangerous." Those words tilted the world, making the ordinary become extraordinary. I held each gem and marveled at moments that piled into years.

Ten years passed since we became husband and wife. We built a strong home. We "settled," and it was a good settling.

One night, looking into the bathroom mirror during our evening routine, I saw our same faces with ever-so-slightly-wrinkled laugh lines in the corners of our eyes. Jonathan's pocket protector with pens lay on the bathroom counter and his white shirt lay out of the edge of the dry cleaning bag. There, leaning forward on the sink with tiny scissors in his hands, Jonathan peered into the mirror, trimming his closely-kept black beard. Watching him with my head slightly cocked to one side, I brushed my long hair in sweeping strokes. Comfortable familiarity permeated the room.

Yet a strange discomfort hung around the edges of the space between us. I knew what it was. I'd been thinking about that conversation at the river. "Two or three children….Maybe we'll adopt someday…God will let us know…."

"Jonathan?"

"Hmmph?" He didn't want to talk while trimming.

I hesitated. He kept trimming. I looked at the clock on the wall. "It's 9:15."

The only movement was Jonathans eyes looking at the clock and then back again, not missing a beat. "Mm-mm. Nope. It's 9:14." I saw a tiny quirk of a smile on the corner of his mouth and laughed.

"9:15, 9:14, yeah, yeah, whatever." Still smiling, I asked, "Do you think the boys are asleep? Should we check on them?"

Jonathan smiled and put the scissors down. Turning and leaning on the counter, he crossed his arms and smiled.

"What is it, Elle? The boys are asleep. You know they're fine. We just checked on them."

Oh, he knew me so well.

"OK. It's not the boys. I've been thinking."

"Yeah?" He listened intently, as he often did.

"Of adoption. I can't get the thought out of my mind. Remember talking about it?"

He nodded.

"It's the thought of a child, somewhere on the face of this earth, without a mom or dad to hold them, that keeps haunting me. The child is alone. Feeling desperate. Living without love. It's weighing heavily on me." My throat felt tight and sore as the words strained out.

Jonathan nodded. "Let's pray about it."

And we did.

A couple of days later, with both of us in the kitchen making lunch, Jonathan touched my arm. I looked up to see him looking at me with that familiar twinkle.

"If we're going to adopt a child," he stated, "we ought to do it now, while you're young and have the energy."

The corner of my mouth lifted wryly. I nodded, adding, "Yeah, before you're too old."

That afternoon, I bought the Journal.

I felt both wonderful and strange. I felt like I'd just opened a door and boldly stepped out – into a dark room. And in that darkness, I immediately felt a need for some sense of control. Maybe it was the fact that I really had no idea what was ahead, and that unsettled me. I have to admit: I jumped in the car and drove to the corner store to buy this simple, brown-covered Journal because I felt powerless, and I had to take some kind of action. I had to do *something*. Deep in my heart, I knew that I wanted to keep track of the whole process. For me. And for my future child.

Returning home from the corner store, I turned the car onto our long wooded drive and glanced at the Journal peeking out of the white plastic bag on the passenger's seat. The blank book stared back.

It seemed to be saying, "So, tell me, Elle...Tell me..."

Inside the house, with car keys put away and Journal pulled from the bag, I sat in the reclining chair in the family room. Arms resting on my legs, holding the Journal in front of me, I flipped the empty pages.

This Journal and I had something in common. We were both waiting. Waiting to walk through the story together. And anxious to complete the pages, to be at the end of the story. That would only happen in measured time.

I opened the book and wrote.

God, help me through this new time. I don't know what's ahead. To say that I'm excited and anxious all wrapped up together doesn't even begin to explain all of what's racing around inside of me. All I know is that adopting a child right now is "right." It's right to do, and it's the right time. Direct me and guide me. Walk with me. Help me. Help our family to become complete.

Our child is waiting. Show us.

Take us to our child.

Chapter Four

The Home Study

So....We decided to adopt. Now what do we do? Where do we begin? It was like the moment of true dark meeting the first sliver of arriving dawn. Squinting your eyes, trying to see the right path to walk on, nothing's perceptible yet.

How in the world do we decide which way to go? Domestic or international? Boy or girl? Newborn or older child? We peered this way and that, trying to distinguish features and distinctiveness to paths, imagining the feeling of our feet pressing into the ground if we chose that particular way.

Then we remembered the story of Jonathan's father's family. Jonathan's German grandparents lived in Russia, struggled in Russia, and diligently tilled their lives in Russia. All conversations turned us to Russia. I found myself imagining that path more often.

I knew we needed to find an agency to provide that proverbial "white glove" home study.

Well, I thought, picking up the phone book and flipping through the Yellow Pages, *I'll start here and "let my fingers do the walking."*

In our small town, I didn't find many listings. *Lutheran Adoption Services is close. That's as good a place as any, I suppose.*

I dialed to set an appointment.

While talking to the receptionist, feelings of intimidation and excitement tickled my stomach…kind of like going up the first hill on a rollercoaster.

No, it wasn't quite like a rollercoaster. It was more like the anticipation felt while walking into a waiting room to be prepped for the intrusive surgery of the home study. Time became injected with an anesthesia that made seconds stretch elastic and undulate into slow motion minutes.

I started feeling prickly with self doubt.

Do we earn enough money? What if they don't like me? I already have two children; what if they don't allow me any more? At night, in fuzzy consciousness, the questions poked me from under the mattress, making me toss and turn.

But I needn't have worried. When we met with our caseworker Lois, all fears fell away. I think it was because she reminded me of my grandmother: White hair done up with care, melodious blue eyes, and creamy voice stirred with kindness and gentleness. Lois emanated wisdom, and I felt comfortable.

Well, as comfortable as you can feel when someone's probing into the most intimate details of your life.

We met with Lois a number of times over the next three months. Like the first time, sometimes we met together in her office. Other times, Lois came to our home. We filled out all kinds of papers and charts, including family history. Sitting in Lois' office, Jonathan spilled stories of the family tree and his grandparents' heritage.

"Jonathan," crooned Lois, "The Russian judge will love this info. Make sure you share these details when you appear in court."

We have to appear in court?

"Tell me, Jonathan, about your siblings." That took a while.

Then Jonathan paused. "My mom died of a heart attack when I was ten." Lois looked up from her scribbles.

Jonathan cleared his now-thin voice. Lois' steady and kind eye contact didn't flicker. I reached over and touched the back of Jonathan's hand and let my fingers press into his with a bit of weight.

Why do we have to go through this? This stranger is lifting back the skin of our most intimate feelings. If everyone who birthed a child had to go through this….

Lois' voice interrupted my thoughts. "Elle, it's your turn. Tell me about your family."

I decided to dive right in.

"I had a pleasant life with loving parents. My dad got cancer and three years later, he died. I was almost nine." *There. It was out.*

Lois sat quietly in her straight-backed, wooden chair. I fidgeted on the somewhat-sunken-in couch.

In a strong urge to fill the silence, I continued.

"A month before my 10th birthday, my mom remarried. My step-dad had a son, Charles, and a daughter, Cheri. We became a blended family." Silence pushed the walls.

"Then I met Jonathan at college."

Ok, so my life didn't blurt and blip out like that. But in those bizarre moments, that's all I could think of. I paused and then spoke again, this time filling in a few details. Lois "um-hm-d" and "yes-d" while scratching the paper with her pen. She seemed satisfied. Then Lois scooched her chair a few centimeters toward us. Now Jonathan's hand pressed down on the back of mine.

"The fact that you've both experienced death may help you in parenting your adopted child. Often, when a child gets older, he or she mourns the loss of the biological parents."

I never thought of that.

"Tell me," Lois continued. "Can you accept a child with disabilities?" I nodded and looked to Jonathan to start this slice of the discussion.

Jonathan and I talked at length about this the night before. Now, he and I talked back and forth to Lois in choreographed reply, like a duo on stage dialoguing through the checklist of what we "would" and "wouldn't" feel comfortable with. Even though in agreement together, stating what children we wouldn't accept left a bothersome pebble of guilt in my shoe. I knew I'd have to take that thought out and look at it later.

Somehow, making these declarations feels like making the decisions of God.

Lois' final question caught me off guard. "Do you have room for another child – Not just in your home, but in your lifestyle?"

I blinked. *Of course.*

On the way home, we rode silently, immersed in thought. Occasionally, one of us placed our ponderings out into the air in a single sentence. The other responded in a phrase or two. Then we sat quietly, the rise and fall of the car's engine the only sound as we pondered again. Emotionally drained, the wheels rolled us home like a gurney rolling us into recovery.

The surgery did its work. We searched our thoughts and began to settle into decisions. Michael was five years old and Thomas was three; we wanted to keep the birth order. I have to admit, most of Lois' input influenced us to choose to adopt a baby.

When it came to deciding whether or not to adopt a boy or girl, I stated the obvious: "We already have boy stuff."

But again, after talking together with Jonathan, Lois' earlier words shaped the outcome: "Your boys are so close. They enjoy each others' company immensely. Perhaps another boy might feel 'left out.' A girl, on the other hand, might have other interests…and since she's a girl, she's already different…."

We decided to adopt a baby girl under one year of age.

There. Our steps pressed down onto a path. The earth felt springy. In the new day's light rising, our eyes started picking out details. Not keen details, by any means. But outlines. Shapes. Direction. Something deep in my chest opened in defenseless abandon toward the wisp of this little unknown child. God lifted a slender branch and gently grafted it into my soul.

A strong desire rose up from the steps into the soles of my feet, through my legs, through my arms, into my hands and finger tips. It was a thirsty, craving desire to inscribe it all, to etch the moments in solid engraving.

I opened my Journal.

Hello, my daughter, my little sweetheart. I can't get you out of my mind. I think of you all the time now. Are you growing strong inside of your mama? I pray she's eating well and taking care of you. I feel an awful ache in my heart for her. I know she must love you very much. She's going to make a great sacrifice . . . a very selfless act. She's giving us an indescribable gift: The precious gift of you.

At that same time, in a small dark room, a woman cried in pain as a little girl arrived into the world.

Chapter Five

Paperwork, Paperwork

Lois let us know that once we had our home study in hand, we could choose any agency across the US to help us find our child. So in between meetings with Lois, I plunged into the Internet to research agencies facilitating Russian adoptions.

Oh my gosh, there were so many! Pushing through the waves of who's who, how they work, and what they were like to work with....I just kept pressing, pointing and clicking.

Days moved along a bit faster than before. I didn't think about my Journal much; there was always something to do, some Internet site to check out, some agency info to read. After the morning routine, with the boys settled into an activity, I'd throw out the Internet net and drag it in again with more info. Sifting through the catch and keeping what looked good, I poured over pages, voraciously devouring words. Driven to find our child, I ate information day after day but never felt "full."

Every once in a while, at night, sitting in my soft chair, I decided to write in my Journal. Words tried to fill the hungry ache.

I never realized there were so many things to do – and so many ups and downs – in adopting a child. I'm so glad we have Michael and Thomas. They are so precious to us. If the adoption falls through, we continue on with life and with our boys. But I pray this adoption goes through, and we do find a beautiful, healthy baby girl. Every day, thoughts of my baby flow in and out of my mind. All I can do is put my energy into making it all happen.

Discovering the agency's personality and particulars felt like a series of first dates; after the first one, you knew whether or not you wanted to go on together. After days of gathering, reading, and often talking with Jonathan long past dark, we decided to sign on and make the commitment with a well-known Christian agency.

Once again, a new part of the path illuminated before our feet. We stood on the path and our emotions rested a moment. Little did we know: The pace was just now picking up.

Shortly after signing a contract and making our first payment, the agency assigned Cindy as our caseworker. I knew the relationship with Cindy would be an important one. Her job was to guide us through the entire process, leading our steps and walking us through every inch of the journey – and even beyond, into three years of post-adoption reports.

To start it all off, Cindy's agency packet arrived in the mail, thick and daunting. Within seconds of emptying the envelope, the bottom line became clear: We needed a boatload of documents. Pages and lists stared at me and then started talking to me all at once. I wanted to cover my ears to take away the overwhelming din.

But instead, I took a deep breath, shushed it all, and began sorting, making mental checklists to create order.

Immigration and Naturalization's 171-H form carried the authority to proclaim with trumpets to all nations that we held permission to bring our child to the US.

Medical reports from our local doctor touted the fact that our blood pumped and our lungs heaved with reliable assurance; yes, we should live well past tomorrow.

Income letters from banks waved dollar signs and exposed our accounts.

Proof of home ownership assured the existence of our walls and roof.

The certified copy of our Marriage Certificate and everyone's Birth Certificates proved our family officially living and breathing together.

Police Clearances confirmed we weren't criminals.

Passports opened the door to travel.

Tax forms lined up files of assurance of our track record of reliable income and the ability to support ourselves.

A Power of Attorney statement placed our signature into a stranger's pen hold.

And we had to be fingerprinted and checked by the FBI.

The FBI!

Our local police department couldn't do our fingerprints, so we had to make a two hour trip to Detroit to "main headquarters." Jonathan took the day off work. Instead of dreading the trip, we decided to make the best of it, to use the car time as moments to speak of our dreams of the upcoming trip overseas. It more than helped pass the time; it focused our mood on why we started the marathon in the first place: our daughter.

Standing in the stark government office in front of the looming fingerprint machine, the white-shirted officer firmly gripped the length of my single finger between his wide fingertips. One by one, each digit endured the rolling motion, pressing my dry, cracked fingers onto the screen.

"Ma'am, we'll have to do three of your fingers again." His military voice sounded matter-of-fact. "Your fingers are too dry, and the print's not coming through."

While Jonathan sat on the molded plastic chair and watched, the officer handed me a plastic bottle of lotion. Rubbing the cream into my hands with deliberate, pressed squeezes, I handed the bottle back, standing expectantly.

"You'll want to wait a while and let that soak in. You can have a seat." I looked at Jonathan, who nodded and smiled, motioning for me to come and sit next to him. Parched seconds ticked by. It sure felt like a government office.

The next time the officer's hands guided and rolled each of my fingers, I watched a clear maze appear for each finger's touch. At the top of the screen, "Conner, Elle," plainly stated ownership of the spiraling circle pictures.

"Perfect. You're finished. You have a nice day." Yes, finished with one more document requirement. But nowhere near finished with the checklist. Free to go. But not truly free from more "work," more steps.

I sighed and pulled up my boots of resolve and tightened my belt for the continued journey.

A strong pattern emerged in our days. It was a pattern of completing seemingly-never-ending "adoption related tasks." Those tasks took priority over anything that used to be "normal" life. The "new normal" included plodding through paperwork, locating what hoops to jump through, and then jumping through hoop after hoop after hoop. Plod and jump. Plod and jump. For a while there, we didn't have much of a social life. Addressing the hoops seemed much more important. And plodding took so much energy.

The to-do list dwindled, with check marks triumphantly blazoned in "it's complete!" marks across the page. The stack of finished documents to turn back in to Cindy grew taller.

Somewhere in the process of all those papers, it felt like I emerged slowly as if from a dark room, eyes blinking, looking around at my two sons, my home, and my friends. A powerful obsession-like spell – a spell driving me to press through the murky list of documents to get to my daughter – slowly released its grip. A new feeling swelled across me with intensity: Desire.

It was a desire to know my new daughter, to see her, to hold her, to touch her hair, to kiss her forehead, to stroke her cheek with my fingertip, to smell her baby breath, to press her gently to my breast while rocking, swaying, and comforting her cries. This desire grew as an itch unable to be scratched, ardent in its longings.

Jonathan could feel it in me. He saw it in my distant looks while standing at the sink and rinsing dishes with long, lazy strokes. He heard it in my musings at meals, remembering baby foods and bottles with Thomas and Michael. He touched it when we stood at the department store table and I held out the white-and-pink terry sleeper to admire.

My Journal started calling to me. Or maybe it called all along, and now I heard its voice more distinctly. Maybe Desire talked with the Journal, conspiring to meet. And when all three of us met, Desire flowed onto the pages of my Journal in messages to my daughter.

My daughter, I think about you many times throughout the day. Your daddy and I talk together about you; we keep trying out different names for you. We want to keep your heritage alive, so we're thinking about the name "Alexandria." Your oldest brother, Michael, likes the middle name of "Rose." My grandmother's name, Sharon, means Rose. We're thinking about some other names too, like Isabelle and Olivia. I'm realizing you may already have a Russian name. I think you are going to be very gentle and beautiful. We'll know what to call you when we meet you. We so want to meet you.

Remembering an article in our local newspaper about a couple who adopted a baby girl from Russia, Jonathan said, "You should call that family that was in the newspaper and see if they'll talk to us about their experience. What were their names....Wasn't it the Bonner family? Rob and Maggie or Molly or something? Didn't you clip that article and save it?"

I didn't have to be convinced. I moved to the newspaper article – and to make the call.

Chapter Six

Personal Connection

After the fourth ring, a soft, professional voice answered. "Hello?"

I got right to the point.

"Hi there. My name is Elle Conner. We live in the same city. My husband and I are adopting a child from Russia, and we read your family's story in the paper about you and your daughter, Kaitlyn Alexandria."

"Oh yes." A smile came through in her words. "It's amazing, how many people saw that article."

"We were wondering if you would be willing to share some information about your adoption experience with us…"

Words barely leaving my lips, Molly answered, "Oh, sure! We're more than happy to! So – how far along are you, in your adoption process?"

"Oh, we just began."

Her question – the equivalent of what everyone asks when you're pregnant: "How far along are you?" – felt funny. Our due date is open-ended, hanging suspended in mid-air on some blank calendar square in the nebulous future.

We didn't talk long – maybe 10 or 15 minutes. But it was amazing at how fast I felt a connection with this woman. And you know what? This woman whom I just "met" eagerly invited us to come over to her home the following week.

Seven long days passed. Jonathan and I dropped the boys off at his mom and dad's and drove to the Bonner's ranch-style house on the other side of town. Striding to the door, we suddenly stood still together, looking at the entrance. The wind made playful noises in the leaves by the porch. I knocked; Jonathan slipped his arm around me. We both waited, feeling small.

A middle-aged woman with blonde hair and hazel eyes swung the door open and smiled. Her soft, pressed white blouse matched her soft, pale skin. "Hello! Welcome! I'm glad you're here! I'm Molly...." Molly's cleanly-articulated words flittered on the air as she delicately swung an arm of welcome and ushered us in.

The first thing we saw, smack-dab in the middle of the living-room floor, was a hardy, stout man with a kind, round face lying flat on his back. A petite two-year-old balanced and bobbled on his legs and his booming laugh swept upwards in concert with his broad movements. The little girl's delicate body and brown hair reminded me of a miniature Russian gymnast, and her thin-yet-strong body giggled, held high in daddy's arms.

Molly laughed.

"And this is Rob – and Katie." Rob flashed a genuine smile toward us and continued to romp while Katie giggled and squealed in delight. Tumbling off her daddy, Katie ran over to grab Molly's knee. Smiling, she leaned over toward me swinging on Molly's leg as if it were a playground pole. Molly reached down to touch her hair. Rob climbed up from the floor with an oomph and stood upright.

I noticed his proud-daddy gaze.

Within minutes of shaking hands, we found ourselves deep in conversation about their personal adoption experience. I remember thinking that most people would be annoyed at our obviously-personal questions; but Molly and Rob's voices showed honest excitement for us, as if honored to prepare us for the months ahead.

"Would you like some tea, Elle?" Molly held herself upright, bringing to my mind the newspaper's mention of her job as a librarian.

Talking about the Detroit Lions, Jonathan and Rob meandered downstairs. Katie's happy tittering sounded sugary and light around their deep voices.

In the kitchen, Molly filled a tea pot with water from the tap, placed the pot on the stove, leaned against the counter, and started sharing the story of their adoption journey. Although she didn't begin with "Once upon a time," her words tumbled into the room like a fairy tale. I listened, nodding….mesmerized, breathing the atmosphere of her every word.

"Here. I have something to show you." Molly led me to the living room couch and patted the cushion for me to sit. Placing her cup of tea on the polished wooden end table, she picked up a small box from around the edge of the couch.

"I want to show you some treasures from our trip to Arkhangelsk."

Cradling the tea cup in my hands, I leaned slightly forward on the edge of the cushion, knees almost touching the coffee table – trying not to look as anxious as I felt and failing miserably, I'm sure of it.

Molly placed the cardboard box in front of us and peeled back the flaps. Reaching in, she carefully drew out a wooden doll about the size and shape of a Bartlett pair. Its smoothness shone in the window light, reflecting painted brush strokes of gold, red, and black.

"Beautiful," I whispered.

"Yes, it is. It's a Matryoshka. They're stacking dolls. See?" Molly gently twisted the wooden base and lifted it to expose another delicately-painted wooden doll the same as the first, but smaller. Then again, and again, she opened the bigger doll, stacking the new little ones in descending order in front of us.

"May I?" I pointed to the smallest one.

"Oh, of course!" Picking up the tiny doll, she placed it in my open hand. I could barely feel the weight of the wood.

Then Molly drew out a small black lacquered box with a white design, its intricate carvings rich in heritage. The top lifted to expose straight, polished inside walls. Then up from Molly's fingers rose a small, hand-carved wooden bird.

How exquisite.

Our visit flew by like the invigorating moments of a delightful party. Standing at the door to leave, Katie ran up and threw her little arms around me in a squeeze, and Molly leaned over to give a tender hug. I felt a bond, a kinship. I didn't want to leave; my heart wanted more.

In the car on the way home, waves of overwhelm rolled over my mind. Each swell receded in feelings that held the shadows of a kind of depression. The path seemed so long. Playing with my daughter as Rob played, feeling my daughter throw her arms around me in a hug – it all seemed so far away. The hazy, indefinable sense of time bothered me, stirring up anxiousness with the feelings of losing control.

Again, in those moments, my Journal breathed my name. Its presence pulled me.

That night, with the boys in bed, I climbed into my big chair. As usual, Jonathan had gone back to work.

I sighed. The routine of every night – Jonathan's coming home for dinner, wrestling with the boys, putting them in bed at eight o'clock, and then returning to work until 11 – felt passive and unsettling at the same time.

Everything's so quiet.

Next to the chair, the Journal peeked its top edge out of the wicker basket.

Yes. I know you're there. Wait a moment. I have to think.

Curling knees up to my chest, I wrapped my arms tightly around them in a hug. Lamplight fell next to the chair. All else lay draped in gray shadows. I closed my eyes. I began rocking, thinking, imagining my daughter, my child.

Questions surged from the shadows.

Who is taking care of her? What is she doing? Is she alright? Why can't I just have her in my arms? Why do others so flippantly become pregnant and carry their child, their precious gift, in nonchalant unawareness… Complaining of feeling so fat, grumpily telling everyone around them what a bother it is to have to wear pregnancy clothes? Don't they know? Don't they understand how fortunate and blessed they are to have their child?

Tears of longing silently wet my cheeks.

I looked at the Journal again. *What can I say to you? I struggle to get these feelings out into words.*

The Journal looked at me again.

I spoke aloud. "I know I can say anything to you."

"*Yes, you can,*" it seemed to say.

But I struggle with finding the right words. This desperate feeling – that I can't do anything right now – I feel so powerless. My friends don't know what to say. They have no idea what it's like to go through adoption. And if I spoke these things, there's no way they could relate... They'd probably feel uncomfortable... and they might even think I was being obnoxious or something. The inner conversation had fun in my mind.

"I'm a Journal. It's not like I'm going to say, 'Well, that was rude!'"

I smiled through the tears.

Yes, Journal. You are my confidant. When no one is able to listen, you listen.

I laughed at myself. I knew the Journal wasn't really talking; in the anxiousness of the moment, I thought a flicker of silliness might chase away the questions. It sort of worked. And sort of didn't.

I picked up the Journal and began to write.

It's so hard to be patient. I don't know you yet, my daughter, but you seem so real. With every event, your daddy and I comment what it might be like next year, when we're a family of five instead of four. It will be so wonderful to hold you, my baby girl, and give you all the love and care that you should have. That every child should have.

Michael and Thomas are so excited about having a sister. I know they're going to be such loving brothers. Already, my daughter, you are so loved. In fact, the entire Conner and Smith families are anxiously awaiting you, Alexandria Rose.

I await you.

I paused. My throat tightened. Tears began to flow down my cheeks again. In my mind, I "spoke" again.

Journal, you have to be my interpreter. You have to be the one to hand over my feelings to my daughter.

I wrote again.

We have to go through so much to get to you. I can't describe to you how much I want you home. With your brothers, I carried them with me. I knew where they were, that they were safe. I did everything I could to make sure they grew strong and healthy. I ate well. I exercised. But if I do that now, it's not doing you any good! Now, the emptiness under my ribs is vast. The frustration is so strong. And the longing for you is palpable.

My pen held suspended above the page. There was only one answer to the emptiness, the frustration, and the longing. The pen's tip pressed to the paper.

Until it's time, God will hold you in His palm.

Chapter Seven

The Real Waiting Begins

When our completed home study arrived in the mail, there's only one word to describe it: Relief – with a capital "R." Pulling open the large envelope, my tummy tickled in excitement. Like a skipping stone across water, my eyes happily skimmed and bounced over rows of words.

We "passed"!

The first major step of our adoption process – absolutely complete!

"Woo-hoo!" I called out.

Immediately making a copy for the second agency, I drove to the post office with the boys to put it in the mail. Completing the first agency's work, this moment was the passing of the baton. What a glorious moment!

Back home, I settled the boys onto the floor with toys and called Cindy.

I loved Cindy's voice. It's not whiny or thin; it's not slow or fast; it's not raspy or thick. It's just a normal, mid-range voice.

Over nine months of working with Cindy, I never met her. Oh, I saw her picture. She kind of looked like her voice; a photo showed her as a single young 25 years old, long blonde hair. . . . Perhaps not a likely person to coach people through building a family. But she knew her job well.

Over the next months, Cindy and I spent a lot of time together on the phone. Touching bases weekly, Cindy's calm tone quickly became familiar and comforting.

How could this young gal empathize with me so well?

To this day, I still wonder.

Over the next days and weeks, we continued to traipse through the second agency's bends and angles of the paperwork maze, including the recommended Hepatitis B vaccinations, with a series of pokes in my arm taking months. Though getting shots isn't my favorite thing to do, I never minded these "inconveniences."

We also took a trip with our stack of completed documents to Michigan's capitol to the Office of the Great Seal. Each and every document needed an "Apostille" – a fancy stamp and raised seal that made the paperwork official and accepted overseas. Each and every necessary task drew us closer to our baby.

Finally, the faithfully-completed paperwork flew FedEx overnight . . . to sit on the desk of a translator for the Russian government.

Now we *really* waited....for "The Referral."

The referral is the name for the file of information on a specific child, including the birth record (if there was one), medical history (if there is any), photos (well, at least one photo), and (if you're lucky) a short video.

My Journal – my daily place to pour out the frustrations of waiting – kept me going. And so I wrote….

Dear Journal,

It's January. It's cold outside, snowing and blowing. It's so hard to be patient. I keep asking God that the first video we receive will be of our child – that we don't have to turn anyone away. I can't imagine looking at a video of a child and saying "no" to any little one in need. One adoptive family I spoke with yesterday told me that they turned down three referrals of children before they felt they'd seen the "right one" – their baby. I can't help but think that I'd feel awfully guilty to do that.

Cindy told us that she believes God directs children to the right families . . . so if we receive a referral that doesn't feel "right," then God has other plans.

"Other plans," I thought out loud.

During the day, it got to the point where I had to do something – anything – to keep busy.

Many soon-to-be moms go through a phenomenon called "nesting." Have you heard of it? It's where the mom "gets the nest ready for the new baby bird" by rearranging furniture, getting baby rooms ready, picking out clothes, and that kind of thing. Even though I didn't physically carry our child, I really do consider that waiting time as "being pregnant without the belly."

And I was definitely nesting.

I decided to rearrange bedrooms, to make room for our coming little one.

Michael and Thomas had separate bedrooms, but most nights, one snuck into the other's room and crawled in bed with his brother. Often, just after walking down the hall from tucking both boys in separate beds, I'd hear a high-pitched voice chirp, "Hey Mikey – will you come over into my bed?"

The answer was always the same: "Sure."

Later, on my way to bed, when peeking through the open slit of Thomas's room, I spied the two of them, snuggling nose to nose, each holding their special teddy bears. I didn't have the heart to move them back to their separate rooms.

I had a plan.

"Hey guys?"

Both boys played with little toy cars on the carpet. I sat down on my heels next to them.

"What, Mommy?" Michael answered.

"What room do you think should be your new little baby sister's room?"

The cars kept zooming. I sat down all the way, cross legged, onto the floor.

"I don't know," peeped Thomas.

"If Grandpa Casey made you guys a set of bunk beds, would you guys room together in Thomas's bigger room, so the baby could sleep in a room by herself?"

It didn't take long for them to answer. "Yeah! Bunk beds! Woo-hoo!"

That was easy.

And Grandpa Casey felt honored. He set right out to build beautiful oak beds for the boys. I could tell it wasn't just a job; it was a labor of love for helping bring home his new granddaughter.

With the beds complete, it didn't take long for me to get to work on the nursery. Finally – something womanly in this masculine house! The smell of peach-colored paint burned my nostrils, and I kept thinking of my little girl one day filling the space with her "girlie things." I had fun dragging the blue-green plaid rug into the boys' new room and rolling out the floral white one in its old place.

At the end of the week, I stood on the step ladder to place sheer peach cloth over the curtain bar with care. Leaning back, nodding in pleasure, two sweet words left my lips: "Very feminine."

In the evening before going to bed, I always kept a baby monitor on, while downstairs. Even though the boys were older, the monitor became my lifeline to hear that all was OK. That night, the sound of giggling poured out of the monitor in cascades of bubbles.

Jonathan and I started a new routine. Every single night, with both boys tucked cozy in their bunk bed within the sheets, we prayed together to ask God to send His angels to protect our little one so far away. Then Jonathan went back to work. And I went to the big chair in the family room to meet with my Journal.

Yes, every night I wrote. I had to. Words poured out. My Journal and I no longer dabbled in thoughts. We had a friendship. Jonathan didn't really understand my feelings – and he couldn't. He's a guy. My friends couldn't understand. They never went through an adoption. And I couldn't call Molly every night. But my Journal – Ah, my Journal was always there. My Journal accepted my questions. My journal never judged. My Journal let me ramble and run on until I could ramble and run on no more. My Journal allowed me to explore the experience and make sense of it all.

And so I wrote:

What will it be like, to have a little one around the house again? It really hasn't been that long since the boys were little . . . and they grew up so, so quickly! I definitely need to baby-proof this house.

I'm sure it'll be chaotic when Jonathan and I return from Russia and try to fit into our "old routine." Hmmm . . . "routine." That will be out the window. *It'll be a whole new kind of routine, if any routine at all. I need to place that time into God's hands.*

I've placed every other detail into God's hands: where the boys will stay when we're gone; flying and the trip over there; how we'll manage in Russia on our own; dealing with foreign food and drink; how long we'll have to stay . . . I can't help but try to imagine what it'll be like over there. I've searched our local library for books on Russia, to study the culture a little, to know what the buildings are like and which buildings we should see while there. I want to appreciate my daughter's home country. Moscow looks like a beautiful place. I wonder how long we'll be there.

I'm sure that seeing the orphanage and babies inside will be tough. What does an orphanage really look like inside, anyway? I can't fathom looking into the eyes of those little children. I don't know how I'll handle it.

This writing helps me sort all my questions out. With the boys in bed and Jonathan at work, I need these moments. Pondering layers upon more pondering.

Adoption is such a strange thing. When I was pregnant, a lot of other women felt they had the right to tell me all their horror stories about labor and delivery. Now, with adopting, people feel they're entitled to tell any and all horror stories about someone they know who adopted. We've heard so many sad stories about illness, lack of medication, poor nutrition, and babies who are sick or even die. My mom's worried about that. And sometimes, if I'm truthful with myself, I'm scared about it, too. I pray for my baby's health every day, many times a day.

Eyelids heavy, I closed the Journal. A red indentation pressed into my finger where the pen had pushed.

Yes, I thought. *Enough of my soul's water colors are brushed onto the page for tonight.*

I'll write more tomorrow.

Chapter Eight

Ups and Downs

Journal,
Today we received our Cable 37. That's the response to our 171-H form for Immigration to allow us to adopt and bring a child across a border and into the US. The Cable arrived in the mail, straight from the American Embassy in Moscow. A woman named Tatiana signed it. It says, "Approved to adopt 1 baby girl under the age of 12 months from the country of Russia."

There. It's official. One more major step, all taken care of.

You know, I wasn't really worried that we wouldn't get this approval – that we wouldn't be accepted.

My hand rested on my knee. I rolled the pen in my fingers. Then the pen settled back against my thumb.

OK. I guess I was a little worried. Not being accepted is always a possibility. If I really think about it, this is a huge step forward.

The tip of the pen hung at the end of the sentence. Then it moved to the next line.

Cindy called today and left a message on our answering machine. She doesn't have a referral for us, but her message said she has some "good news" to tell us. It's killing me that I have to wait until tomorrow to find out what the "good news" is. I hope there's a little girl out there waiting for us, right at this moment. God, I pray we find her soon.

I paused again. Molly and Rob's words about their own trip to Russia floated into my mind. Thoughts and ideas mixed with my dreams and feelings, drawing and swirling themselves into pictures and misty movie-like clips of my imaginings, and I saw myself in Russia holding a nameless, faceless child. The image dissipated, and I moved slowly back from the world of contemplation to write again.

It would be nice if our daughter was in Arkhangelsk, since Molly and Rob are familiar with that area. What a special bond our girls would have.

My pen stopped. What would be the chances of that happening?

The next day, from the moment my eyes opened, I watched the clock. The agency wouldn't answer phones until nine o'clock. I tried to wait to call Cindy until 9:30 AM or so, but I ended up calling at 9:05.

"Hi Cindy – I got your message yesterday. What's the news?" I'm glad she couldn't hear my heart hammering in my ears. The boys toddled through the room, one chasing after the other, completely unaware of my emotions.

"Oh – yes! The news….A new orphanage signed on with us. It's located in Tula. In March, they'll have newborns ready to be assigned. We've been promised the first three girls."

March! That's just weeks away! A thrill ran through my body, leaving the middle of my chest feeling warm.

I never thought of a newborn before. You know, the trip might be a little less traumatic with a really-little one. And she'd probably have a shorter adjustment period, as would the boys.

"You and two other families signed on at the same time. So there are three of you waiting, and it's a good possibility that your referral will be in this bunch. I need you to get a few more documents together. Could you have them back to me by next Friday?"

"Absolutely." I could have the documents there by *this* Friday.

"Once the papers arrive, if all looks good, they'll send a video of a baby."

Her words lingered.

The video: The moment of seeing a child…maybe *our* child. It felt like the moment when you haven't eaten all day, and you're setting the table with plates full of delectable delights and want to taste the food *so badly.*

We spoke just a little more, Cindy promised she'd phone us the second she received more news, and I ended the call feeling pulled along a few more inches on the string of this whole adoption experience.

Oh, why do we have to wait so much?

That afternoon, Jonathan took the boys to the park while I filled out the new paperwork. Watching my husband walk out the door, all dressed to play in his blue jeans and down coat with two rumbly-tumbly boys in snowsuits, I couldn't help but imagine him holding a sweet little girl dressed in pink.

Three days later, Cindy called again.

"Apparently, the facilitator in Russia went to the new orphanage to tape the referral video, and the orphanage nurse turned him away at the door. The entire baby home is under quarantine due to an outbreak of the measles or chicken pox or something major — we're not sure what."

I sat down in the chair, silent, phone cold and hard against my ear.

Another delay.

After the call, I grabbed the Journal and plopped down in the big chair.

All right — I can't get depressed about this. I know that when I get my mind set on something, I focus, focus, focus, and do all I can to put all of my energy into reaching that goal. But this is not in my control. This is not up to me. I absolutely need to be patient. I need to understand that GOD is in control, and that HE has a plan. In HIS timing, HIS plan is revealed.

Within a few short days, the phone rang again. Cindy told us the referral from Tula fell through. It wasn't going to work out — at all.

Journal, I'm so frustrated! I don't know why this is happening — why there's another delay. I keep praying things will settle down and we'll find our daughter. I want to love her and care for her needs. God — it's so hard to wait. I'd love to have some answers — right now.

Stopping for a moment, I realized my breath came out fast and short. My hand pressed back into the page.

Where is she? What does she look like? What will it be like to have her grow up here? What will she grow up to do in her life? What's our family going to be like? God, what's Your purpose for our family?

Fighting thoughts punched and pushed out onto the page.

And God, why couldn't our daughter-to-be stay with her birth mother? Is her birth mother grieving at all? Does she weep for her child? How many mothers in that country weep for their children? Do they feel the loss? Are they numb, without sensation, feeling deadened inside? For the majority of the families in Russia, everything's so economically poor over there right now. Will things get better for them? Will their children be able to be cared for? Do they know how the desire to love a waiting child burns deep and hot within me here, waiting, waiting, waiting to love a child?

Emotional coals smoldered in my chest.

Days later, Cindy called again.

"We have a referral video of an eight-month-old girl from the region of Irkusts."

My heart leapt forward.

"But I must tell you, the judge in that region is causing court delays. We don't know why, but he closed off adoptions in that region for an un-determined amount of time. We aren't sure when the region will re-open, but you can see the video if you'd like."

My heart doubled back.

"Cindy, I'll talk to Jonathan about it today and call you back."

Staring at the receiver back in its cradle, I couldn't help thinking, *What's to talk about? What kind of referral would that be? It would be "maybe" having a child, "if" the judge "perhaps" re-opens the region.*

Jonathan and I agreed: We couldn't become involved with this child….for fear we'd never be able to bring her home.

That night, with the boys in bed and Jonathan at work, my Journal and I returned to our familiar place. But the hours of every-day comings-and-goings in between the phone call with Cindy and speaking with Jonathan melted my frustration. This time, letters turned into words with gentle, measured strokes.

Prayer is a powerful thing. I need to rely on that. I've been so busy, first with paperwork and then with trying to get the house prepared, that maybe I've missed it all. Maybe what I should be doing is dropping down on my knees to pray.

I cry easily. All the time. It really is like being pregnant, except when I was pregnant, I could take care of my baby by taking care of myself. Who cares for my baby? Who answers her cries? Does anyone?

Tonight, Thomas came in to the kitchen wearing a big pout. He felt sad about something that was really quite small to me, as a "grown up"; but it was so big to him, as a little one. He ended up crying, and I held him as he cried. My arms wrapped around his little body – and my mind flew far away, distracted by the horrible thought, "Who holds the little children who have no mommies and daddies? Who holds them when they cry?"

God, I pray – no, I plead with you: Send an angel to my child. But God, I pray for more. Much more…Please. Send your angels. Hold each of these children.

And God, more importantly: Send these little ones mommies and daddies to hold them. Give more of us a soul-understanding; let us feel the ache of a little child's alone-ness.

Oh, how Your heart must agonize over Your little ones who are alone.

To be held. What a simple, basic need. And they don't have it.

Life is strange. I can't even begin to figure things out.

When Jonathan came home from work, he found me curled up in the big chair, asleep. He gently pulled the open Journal out from under my hand. Reading the last entry, he closed the Journal and slipped it into the wicker basket beside the chair.

He dropped to one knee. Leaning forward toward the soft leather, he brought his hands to rest onto the arm of the chair. Lacing his fingers together, he pressed his folded fingers against the base of his forehead and closed his eyes.

After some moments, Jonathan's head rose. Letting his fingers unlace to rest on the chair, he looked up at my sleeping face. Reaching forward, he brushed a few strands of my hair aside that had fallen on my cheek. I opened my heavy eyes.

The corner of his mouth pulled back into a gentle smile. Jonathan reached over and clicked off the lamp. Slipping his hand behind my elbow, the two of us rose and walked side by side through the soft shadows and up the stairs to sleep.

Chapter Nine

Wait Upon the Lord

My little daughter, it is now the month of March. Still, I have no word of you.

Michael is seven years old; Thomas turned five. Every day, they ask when you will come. It's so hard not to be discouraged. You're out there somewhere, and I really need to get to you. I'm unreservedly anxious to celebrate your life.

Alexandria, I want to call you "Allie" already. Do you like it? I must speak your name, because it makes you more "real."

Are you old enough to know where you are? Are you aware of your desolate surroundings? I read today that in Russia, where you are, many places don't have enough food. I worry about you. We want to send food and clothing, but we're told that whatever we send won't make it to you. With people so desperate, anything we send will be stolen as soon as it reaches the Russian border.

My thoughts come to you many times a day. All around us, there are so many parents with children. And yet we wait and wait.

They don't know what they have.

I know that God is teaching me to be patient. But I think I'm missing the point. I mean, I know that everything "works out for the best." But right now, in the middle of this whole adoption process, it's hard to believe that waiting is good — for you, for us, or for anyone.

I look at your clothes stacked neatly in your drawers and hanging perfectly in your closet. I glance at the teddy bear border I put up in your room. And my emotions take over.

I'm sick of waiting. I want to do something.

I want to protect you. I know I should feel content that God's protecting you. I should be content in that. After all, He is GOD! But in my humanness, I can't help but feel helpless, like I'm not doing enough.

Molly has been so supportive. She and Katie came over yesterday, and we talked more about their own experiences in Russia. Talking about the trip helps me feel a little more comfortable about traveling. But I have to admit, at this point, after seeing Katie right here, cute as can be, I feel more anxious. I want to see what you look like!

I'm thankful Rob and Molly have Katie. I'm happy for them. They're blessed. And we're blessed, too, with two beautiful boys. I couldn't ask God for better sons. I feel guilty . . . Shouldn't that be "enough"?

The emotions of waiting seep into everything that I do, tainting every moment with the colors of impatience. I never knew that adoption would consume me like this. Sometimes Michael comes up to me and wraps his little arms around my neck and says, "It's OK, Mommy."

Sometimes things just don't feel OK.

Then I read the verse in the Bible, in the second chapter of Lamentations, verse nineteen: "Pour out your heart like water before the face of the Lord. Lift your hands toward Him for the life of your children." I'm pouring and lifting. My heart runs dry and my arms ache.

And then there's the verse in Psalm 139 that says, "I knew you even before I knitted you in your mother's womb." He knows who you are and that you're destined to be with us. You're destined to be my daughter. He knows you, and soon I'll know you.

Most of all, I cling to the promise that's written in the book of the 29th chapter of Jeremiah, verse 11, where it says, "For I know the plans I have for you, says the Lord. Plans for good and not evil."

God's plans are GOOD. I have to trust in those plans. Yes, God is aware of every single second of this adoption process that your daddy and I are going through. God is working through each and every step that brings us closer to you.

And He knows exactly what you're doing right now. His plans are for you to be with us.

He'll make it happen.

Most of all, God knows exactly how I feel. Right now, right here, all of the emotions swirling and twirling and rising up and falling back . . . every single sensation, every single passion, every single mood, and every single concern.

I can't begin to explain to you how much I long for you.

I put the Journal down and opened my Bible to Isaiah 44:2 and read, "I am your Creator. You were in my care even before you were born."

Allie, you are in God's care. We've finished all we have to do here. Everything is in place. It's taken months of phone calls, meetings, and paperwork upon paperwork to get to this moment. All I can do is trust God for the next step.

I will "wait upon the Lord."

Chapter Ten

The Video

Michael and Thomas were "fishing" that afternoon in the family room. Thomas sat in the little plastic baby bath tub (which we'd never gotten rid of) – barely fitting in, mind you, with his little knees sticking up like a fisherman in a shrinking boat. He held the end of a skinny stick plucked earlier that morning from the woods bordering our property. With care, Michael had tied the string onto the twig's end. Now Thomas dangled and waved the "pole" in movements that made the "fishing line" tickle the surface of the living room carpeting. Michael wiggled across the floor, grabbing at the line.

Michael made a great fish.

I'd just lifted a clean baking dish from the cupboard to start making a casserole for dinner when the phone rang.

"Hi, Elle – It's Cindy!"

I tried not to get back on the roller coaster of hopeful emotions that accompanied Cindy's calls. But I couldn't help it. Every time she called, I climbed into the coaster's car, buckled my seatbelt, put down the safety bar, and went up the hill expectantly.

"Hello Cindy. How are you? Any news?" No use trying to be coy.

"I have a video for you. A referral. Of a little girl. This time, it's in a region we're very familiar with. We've worked with them a number of times before. There shouldn't be any issues."

Everything went numb.

For us? You finally have a video for US?

The moment I'd waited for was finally here, and it felt absolutely strange and wonderful and frozen in time. Then, all of a sudden, I had the unmistakable urge to jump in the car and drive those five states between me and Cindy to get the video in my hands.

"I can't send the referral out today; the mail's gone out already. But I'll send the video tape and papers right out to you in tomorrow's mail, express overnight."

Hallelujah!

My voice lilted goodbye, the line clicked, and I called Jonathan.

"We have a referral coming!"

For five minutes, we giggled back and forth like two kids with comments like, "What do you think she's going to look like?" and "I can't wait to see her fingers and toes" and "What color do you think her hair is?"

Then Jonathan stated, "Well, I have to go – I have to finish this quote."

How could he turn it off like that?! I wanted to talk for hours!

After calling my mom and Molly and Sarah and everyone I could think of, dinner and bedtime flew by. My hands moved this way and that, my feet walked this way and that, and my mind wandered thousands of miles away to Russia, wondering about the little girl we were going to see on a video tape so very soon.

Boys in bed, lights out, I grabbed the Journal and sprung into the chair. Flipping out the footrest, I threw my feet up, crossed my ankles in a flair, and whipped out my pen with a flick of the wrist.

Journal, I'm jumping out of my skin! We're supposed to receive our first photos and video referral the day after tomorrow! It's here . . . It's finally here: The time to actually see a child that could be ours. I keep praying over every little detail: The FedEx truck arriving early, the information, our child's health, traveling, our boys, and our family's adjusting . . . Oh, my mind is blowing around in gusts of excitement.

I'm trying to give everything to God. But, I have to tell you, it's difficult to totally place all my worries in His hands and not take them back.

The next day was so, so hard to wait through! I called the agency to make sure the video was sent.

"Yes," said the secretary. It was sent. It went out DHL."

DHL! Not Federal Express?

My heart hit to the floor with a thud.

"But ma'am, DHL doesn't deliver to our area daily!"

Who knows when the package would get here?! What could have been overnight sat now as a great big, lumpy question mark.

The next day, nothing arrived.

And the following day, nothing arrived.

The third day, nothing arrived. I called the DHL office. It was really, really hard not to lose it on the phone.

"Look. Three days ago, our agency sent this video express overnight. That was three days ago. Do you have it?"

The man on the other end of the line sounded a bit perturbed. "Well, we only come to your little town on Thursdays."

Thursdays? What happened to "overnight mail"?! And I think I heard him emphasize the word, "little"....

"Sir, I'll come and get the video. Where are you? I'll meet you somewhere. Anything. Just tell me where to go, and I'll get it."

"I'm sorry, Ma'am. The package has already been loaded onto the truck. There's nothing you can do. You just have to wait until the truck gets to you."

"So when will that be?"

"Ma'am, I can't tell you."

How ridiculous!

Going about the motions of daily living, all I could think about was that darned video sitting on a truck somewhere, about an hour away from our home. Just sitting! Even the boys showed disappointment. And every morning, they asked me, "Is the video coming today?"

Each time I reassured them with a squeezy-hug.

"I don't know. But God knows."

I think I was reminding myself more than telling them.

The next day, I awoke cranky and impatient. It was April 1st. A Monday. The fifth day of waiting.

After the boys left for school, I called the agency in the morning and told them what was up. Cindy wasn't in, but some woman answered and said, "Oh, I've seen that video! She's such a beautiful baby!"

Don't tell me THAT! I want to see for myself! Aargh!

Alright, that was it. Right then and there, I decided I was going to sit, wait, and watch for that stinkin' DHL truck. Yes, I was a little bit crazy with the waiting, because you and I both know that watching won't make anything come sooner. But at that point, I didn't care.

I'd had it.

I sat on the edge of the couch in the living room and turned on the television. With the google eyes of a chameleon, I placed one eye on the morning show and the other eye out to the stone driveway. Every time I heard a car go by, my heart beat went up and I jumped up to pull back the curtains. A dozen or so cars later, my toss of the curtains revealed an unfamiliar truck coming up to our home.

Running out the front door, I couldn't help but think, *this better not be an April Fools Day joke!*

"Do you have a video for me?" The driver, still in his seat, hadn't even stopped his truck yet, as I shouted into his open door.

"Yes, I do."

Yes! Yes! At last!

He reached back into the bundles, opened his door, and stepped out to hand me a package.

I wanted to hug him.

Instead, I thanked him, grabbed the package, and ran inside to call Jonathan to come home from work, so we could view the video together.

Within five minutes, Jonathan drove in, jumped out, and ran to the house. Hands dripping with sweat, my fingers struggled to peel off the sticky sealant.

Oh, forget the sealant! I ripped the top open.

We both peered in. There sat the black plastic rectangle of the video, with all kinds of papers squeezed in next to it.

Jonathan pulled out the video and took it to the VCR player while I pulled out the papers. A medical report. Typewritten papers in English, with all kinds of strange words. Those big words didn't look too good.

The video screen blipped. I immediately placed the papers aside.

We both sat and stared, totally focused on the picture on the screen.

Chapter Eleven

Our Little Girl

The little girl lay on her back in a crib, almost completely still. Her wide eyes stared directly into the video camera. The clean sheets and taught blanket beneath her body stayed meticulously in place, tucked tight to the edges of the crib. For one full minute, the little one barely moved.

And neither did we.

Surges of excitement rose within my chest, wrapping together into a bundle of ache to hold this little one. I tried desperately to blink away the tears of joy and anticipation welling up, so the picture would stay clear. But the wetness forming into crescent pools at the bottom of my eyes made her image bend and swirl.

I searched every inch of the screen, looking carefully for any signs that this child could be ours. She was so real, it was if I could reach into the screen and pick her up.

Then a caregiver entered the picture from the left, with long arms reaching forward to pick up the baby. On cue, the baby puckered her lips to be fed, as if ready for an invisible bottle. The baby's thin arms waved and one foot kicked in expectancy. I marveled at her pale skin.

She's completely beautiful.

Then the video blinked, fuzzed just a second, and the screen went blue.

Immediately I hit the rewind button. While the machine hummed itself back to the beginning of the tape, I turned to Jonathan. He stood with a paper pulled from the package, page gripped between both hands, head forward, peering closely at the paragraphs.

"It says here she was born at 23 weeks gestation." Jonathan pointed at the numbers on the paper. I focused on the words "Medical Report" at the top of the page, and by the time I read the word "weight" a few lines down, Jonathan's numbers-based mind had already translated the metric into the American equivalent.

"And she was born at 3 pounds and…and 3 ounces. Wow, that's small."

I nodded and moved in beside him. He handed me the papers.

The humming tape clicked. Jonathan pushed "play" on the remote.

Looking at the pages before me, I couldn't focus. Emotions kept standing between my brain and the ability to decipher the page. It was if someone stood inside my head, grabbed the words before they "got to me," and tied them all in knots. Though written in English, it felt like I was trying to read a foreign language.

The baby's image came onto the screen again.

Trying desperately to unwrap those strange pretzel words in my mind, I read aloud. "She was in the hospital for two months…Let's see…"

The words "Residence: Arkhangelsk Baby Home," jumped from the page.

"Oh, Jonathan! She's in Arkhangelsk!"

That's where Rob and Molly went!

Emotions clashed: In a flow of joy, the beautiful baby stared at me again through the television screen, while splashes of dread jumped from the paragraphs upon paragraphs of medical words bunching across the page in my hands.

"She has spastic tetraparesis, whatever that is, Rickets Stage II, perinatal lesion of the central nervous system of hypaxial and traumatic genesis, Icteric Syndrome, Bulbar Syndrome, hip dysplasia, and, oh my goodness, Jonathan, a whole list of things I can't even pronounce!"

On the television screen, the little baby kicked.

"This report is a little intimidating." He was quiet a few seconds then shook his head. "But I think it's built up. Cindy *did* say that Russian medicals often sound worse than the child's actual health...."

"Yes, yes," I interrupted. "I remember. But this! Oh Jonathan!"

In silence, we both stared at the screen.

When I spoke again, my voice couldn't hide the inner turmoil. "She doesn't look like she has this laundry list of... of....of so many *problems*."

"I have a sneaking suspicion that they 'go overboard' on information like this so that we can't come back later if something's wrong."

I'm sure he's right. He must be right.

"Elle, let's get out that information that Cindy gave us. You know – those international adoption doctors who view videos and referral documents. Let's get it checked out. Let's see what they say."

Glancing at the baby on the television calmly gazing at the caregiver, I nodded. *This baby certainly didn't look like all of those words on the medical page.*

The video ended again. I rushed from the room to get the list of doctors' phone numbers.

It wasn't a big list. Jonathan and I browsed the names.

"How about this 'Dr. Dana Johnson' at the International Adoption Clinic at the University of Minnesota? The information says he's a 'pioneer' in the field of adoption medicine."

"He looks good. Says here they 'try to assess the health and well-being of a child before a family decides to adopt.' That's what we could use."

I nodded.

With Jonathan at my side, I dialed the phone. A woman answered.

"Medical records are often incomplete or incomprehensible," said the woman on the other end of the line.

I nodded into the phone in agreement. "That's right – There are words we can't even pronounce in this little girl's medical report!"

"Yes, I know." She sounded sympathetic, which made me feel a little better. Just a little bit.

"There are a lot of meaningless labels, like 'pyramidal insufficiency,' that Russian doctors put on the records of all infants born prematurely to impoverished mothers."

Oh my gosh. These words do sound terrible.

"So, you get the video that we have here, and the doctor takes a look at it?"

"That's right."

We talked just a little bit more, and the more we talked, the better I felt. She cited the fact that their specialty has been recognized by the American Academy of Pediatrics and that they worked with Ivy League medical schools. *And* they assessed over 2,000 videos and records a year. Yes, by the end of the call, I felt really good about working with this clinic.

I made copies of the papers and sent everything out in the mail to Dr. Dana before the clock's hands announced mid afternoon. Then I called my mom. And then Molly. And then Sarah. And I think if it wasn't getting so late in the afternoon, I would have called anyone else I could think of.

I knew it was happening. I knew I was falling in love with this little one already.

Before dinner, while the boys played in their room, I pulled out the Journal to inscribe a quick note.

I must have played your video fifty times. You are so beautiful! In these few hours since I first saw you, you've stolen my heart. Our little Russian princess, we'll do all we can to get you home. I pledge my love to you. We pledge our love to you. Forever.

Chapter Twelve

Medical Fears

After putting the casserole in the oven for dinner, I called our family doctor, Carol.

"Carol – It's here…the referral video…."

The words barely left my lips when Carol replied, "Oh Elle – I'm so glad for you!"

I knew the whole town waited for this moment; my breaking news splashed like a rock tossed gleefully into a still pond; undoubtedly, right through the phone line, echoing ripples of excitement began to race across the water's surface. I jumped right in with it.

"Can I come over to show you the video and papers?"

"Of course. Come over right after dinner." With Carol, I expected nothing less. What a great resource – and friend.

At the end of dinner, after gulping in my last bite, I snatched my jacket, said goodbye to Jonathan and the boys, grabbed the video and papers, and jumped into the car. Jonathan's eyes smiled steadily and the boys shooed me out with goodbyes.

I'm so blessed to have those three. Thank you, God! And I'm so glad Carol's willing to take a look at this video...

It wasn't far to go; nothing in our town is. On the way there, I couldn't help but realize that, in many ways, this adoption wasn't just ours; it was the whole town's experience. Right from the start, I'd told everyone of our decision to adopt, always asking, "Please pray for us."

So from the beginning on, someone each and every week asked, "Where are you in the process? When is your baby coming home?"

At first, the constant questions didn't bother me at all. But that moment, driving to Carol's, I realized that every time I walked through town, just about everyone wanted information from me in the form of "new news." Thinking about it now, irritation's prickly pokes rose up my back. People almost seemed bothered by the fact that I had nothing special to say. Didn't they realize that the waiting – and not having any new information – bothered *me?*

When I was pregnant, people wanted to feel my belly. All of us moms know how intrusive that can be. Well, like the belly touching, those moments of asking over and over, "When is the baby coming?" are intrusive too. It's not like people are trying to be intrusive. Other people want new information; but I don't have any. They expect me to know *when* we'll get our baby; but I have absolutely no sense of when it's going to happen.

I know they just want to share in the joy of it all. Yes, they're just trying to be nice. But at night, when I walk into the quiet nursery, I look at the baby clothes folded in drawers; the crib is made up; everything's laid out straight and ready. And the "not knowing" gets worse. I don't know where my baby is. I don't know who's taking care of her – or *if* someone's taking care of her. And above all, I don't know when she's coming. Through the day and every night, I ask myself over and over: *When is she coming?*

It haunts me.

When Molly and Rob adopted Katie, no one knew about their adoption until the article appeared in the newspaper. Now I think I knew why. Privacy.

I looked over at the video on the seat beside me. *I wonder how people will react now that we have a referral – the picture and assignment of an actual child. I wonder if they'll expect me to be able to jump on a plane to go and get her tomorrow. As if I could! Everyone knows so much about our intimate adoption details. Oh, how I wish I had the answers for "when"! Oh, how I wish I could go and get her right now!*

I pulled into the beautiful drive of Carol's grand farm home. The setting sun's shadows reached through the trees, making enchanting patterns stretch across the grass and up to the porch. I followed their trail and knocked on the frame of the screen door.

"Come in!" Carol's voice echoed across the polished wooden floors. Pulling back the door from its thick frame, I stepped in.

Just in her early 30's, Carol behaved like a typical small-town doctor. Open kindness reflected through her smile; she never hid her excitement regarding the novelty of "being in on" our whole adoption process. An attitude of professional veneer didn't exist.

"Come in, Elle. We'll go into the study…" I followed Carol across the airy country kitchen. Once in the study, standing side by side, I handed over the papers and watched while Carol read. Her eyes narrowed. Her lips slowly closed into a line. The home and I stood silent together. The room felt stiff.

"Hmm." That's all she said.

My stomach tightened. The stately home's silence thickened. Each time Carol turned a page, the paper's rustling reverberated through the room. Normally, I loved the warmth of this home; but now, as the last slivers of yellow sunlight disappeared, the grayness through the windows cooled the ambiance of the house. I shifted my weight.

"Elle, let's go into the living room and watch the video." Even though spoken at a normal volume, Carol's words seemed loud.

"Sure. Yes, let's watch. What do you think, Carol? I mean, about the papers. I know there are a lot of words there, and Cindy says that there are usually phrases put on the page that really don't mean anything…"

Carol's face showed obvious concern. "Let's watch the video together."

And when the video played, Carol stood starkly still, staring. Neither one of us spoke. The video finished and Carol turned. She spoke with hesitance, voice nearly shaking.

"Oh, Elle. I don't think this is a very healthy child. She's obviously developmentally delayed. Her left side is, well….too relaxed and still. I'm concerned that she could even be paralyzed on that side. I want to be excited, but to tell you the truth, I'm scared for you."

My chest felt like someone was standing on it. I took in a breath. Carol looked down at the papers in her hand and then back at me.

"It says here she has hip dysplasia. Your home is tri-level. If she can't get around, you might have to move. Do you have any idea what you're doing?"

Defiance rose up into my throat and balls of energy spun in my chest. But my words came out different than the storm raging inside. "Well. I appreciate your honesty. But we do know what we're doing. We know this adoption is the right thing to do. I really don't think she's that bad."

Carol tried to smile but it came out as a frown. I wondered if the squeezing emotions of this tense moment would bruise our friendship. I hoped not.

I didn't say much more. I listened a few more minutes to Carol's explanations and concerns, sincerely thanked her, and left.

In the car, I glanced at my watch; the whole visit lasted only about 20 minutes and felt like hours.

I'll take this all with a grain of salt. Carol's a wonderful doctor…but she's not experienced in international adoption. I'm going to see what Dr. Dana has to say.

At home, Jonathan had already tucked the boys in bed. Sitting on the couch together, I shared Carol's words. He listened intently, eyes steady. In his typical way, Jonathan acknowledged Carol's concern but didn't get drawn into the emotions.

"There's nothing we can do to control it right now. Let's wait and get it checked out with Dr. Dana."

"Yes. I agree."

I wanted to say more about Carol but didn't. Instead, I said, "Let's watch the video one more time before we go to bed."

And while the little one lay there, we watched her little eyes move. As my eyes and body soaked in the essence of this little one, I spoke to Jonathan.

"I admit it."

"What's that?" Jonathan didn't take his eyes off the screen either.

"In my heart, she's mine. This is our daughter."

Jonathan kept his eyes on the screen. "What would anyone see in a video that would cause them not to accept a child?" His words hung in the air.

Then Jonathan spoke again, voice low and steady.

"I don't see anything."

It wasn't that late, but it felt late. The little girl on the screen looked back at us. In a motion I knew so well, the little one kicked her leg. I knew her every next move.

Then the screen went blue.

Jonathan hit the remote button and the television clicked black, joining the stillness. We turned to look at each other.

"Elle," said Jonathan, "this is our child. Let's hear what the doctor says, but let's leave her health in God's hands."

He accepted her for who she was. He accepted it for what it was.

Our referral. Our child.

Any uneasiness hiding in the corners of my being melted away.

"You go on, honey," I said. "I'll be right up to bed. I just have to write something first."

Jonathan smiled, squeezed my arm, and let his fingers slip across my sleeve as he rose. I watched him go and then sat on the edge of the big leather chair.

To my right, my Bible and Journal lay pressed side by side, tucked together in the basket on the floor. I pulled the two books out together. Placing the Bible on top of my lap, I opened it. Flipping the pages, I found Mark 11:24. I slid the Journal up to my other knee and copied from the Bible into the Journal's pages:

Therefore I say to you, whatever things you ask when you pray, believe that you receive them, and you will have them.

Then I wrote underneath:

You are a child of God. Our daughter. Don't ever doubt who you are. While you are apart from us, living in the orphanage, we pray nightly that God will protect you, comfort you. God has a purpose for your life and you must always put your trust in Him. He will take care of you.

Your little life is about to change so much in the very near future.

Chapter Thirteen

Truly Ours

The next morning, with Michael in school, Thomas and I hurried off to Molly's with video in hand. Molly usually worked at the library from afternoon right up to ten o'clock in the evening. I didn't call ahead, because if we went to Molly's first thing in the morning, I knew she would be home. Besides – I wanted to share everything "in person" and with surprise. All the way there, I thought through a number of clever ways to tell her the great news. I couldn't wait to see her face.

Of course, when Molly opened the door, I babbled it right out: "Our referral came – from *Arkhangelsk!*"

Molly flung her arms around my neck and tears wet both our faces. Hooking her arm into mine, Molly led me inside, our words tumbling and bumping into each other.

"Imagine that! What a miracle! God had a master plan, hand-picking two little girls from the same city – on the other side of the world – to live together as friends in a little town of 2,000!" We laughed and marveled and cried some more.

Guiding me to the living room, we watched the video together, and I cried again. Oh, the tears just kept streaming, emotions spiraling and tumbling out. I wanted so badly to reach out and hold this child! Right here, right in front of my eyes, was my baby. In my heart, I knew it. But then I was wondering, too, of the doctor's reports. I wanted everything to be all OK, finished, complete, with her here – not stuck in this slow-motion process with open-ended question marks.

What an absolute blessing to have Molly. She understood.

I turned to look her in the face. "Oh, Molly -- Thank you for sharing your experiences with me! Knowing that you've been through it all and that your daughter is here with you now . . . It keeps me going. It's so *wonderful* to have someone who understands what I'm feeling."

We embraced again.

Molly whispered, "Don't worry. It *will* happen. You *will* bring your daughter home. You're on your way now."

From that day, something changed. My waking moments were not the same.

Before he went to work, Jonathan and I talked what seemed like every second of the video. And then we talked about it again at lunch time. And at dinner. And then again at bedtime. Yes, I admit it: I obsessed about that precious little girl. I returned to the television over and over. During the day, the boys and I talked about it, watched it again, and then played it again and talked about it some more.

The next day was Ash Wednesday. I made a vow to focus on "normal life" and not watch the video so much – and just to *think* about that beautiful little one. As you can guess, that's *all* I thought about.

Time passed ever-so-slowly.

In the mid-afternoon, Thomas and I sat on the floor of his room playing GI-Joes. At this point, I was successfully playing with Thomas and "living in the now," busily moving my guy across the floor in tactical maneuvers. I must say, with Michael at school (and knowing Thomas would soon follow), I cherished these times where the two of us luxuriously dabbled in toys and imaginings.

"How about we have a dinner together," my guy said to Thomas's guy; Thomas had a grip on his guy's back, making him creep across the carpet in typical army-guy strategic crawl.

"C'mon, Mom!" Thomas exclaimed, letting out a little-boy grunt followed by shooting noises. "No talking!" *Oh yeah*, I reminded myself. *This is boy play. No dinners, lots of noises.*

The phone rang. As habit, I automatically moved and deftly gathered a few of the soldiers in my arms, took Thomas's hand in mine and, with Thomas in tow, scooted to my bedroom next door to answer it.

"Hello. This is Doctor Dana." My heart leapt.

Oh my gosh – so soon! And he's calling me himself! I expected a nurse or something...

"Is this Elle Conner?"

"Yes, this is Elle Conner. Dr. Dana, thank you for calling!"

"Yes. I've received a video from you of a little girl..."

I dipped my head down to catch Thomas's attention and, as soon as his eyes met mine, put my pointer finger to my lips in a silent *shhhh*. In seconds, I settled Thomas around the other side of my bed with the toys and quickly flipped on the Public Television's channel – in case the soldiers weren't enough to keep his attention during the call. All the while, Dr. Dana talked, and I tried so desperately hard to focus on his every word.

To hold the anxiousness twirling in my body, I stepped back around to the other side of the bed, lowered myself to the floor, pressed my back against the mattress, and brought my knees up to my chest. Sitting tightly in a ball, I pushed the earpiece to my head, straining to catch his every word and nuance.

"...Russia tends to put a lot of scary words in their paperwork..." His words and tone were strong, brief, sure of himself. "I believe the baby has rickets, but proper nutrition will improve that. There don't seem to be any major signs of health trouble such as Fetal Alcohol Syndrome."

I wondered, *Should I be writing this down? Oh, I don't have time to go get something to write on . . . I want to listen . . .*

"Most institutionalized children are influenced in some way by their early deprivation; some have minor and transitory issues and others have medical and developmental disabilities that will last a lifetime, with a wide range of outcomes . . ."

Yes, I knew this. *Is there a problem...or is he making sure we're realistic in our expectations . . .*

"All in all, from what I see, I believe she will end up being a rather healthy child."

A rather healthy child! I felt like turning cartwheels!

Gratefully acknowledging his time with, "Thank you so much, doctor," I hung up the phone and immediately picked the receiver up again to dial Jonathan's number at work.

My words spilled out in joy, and Jonathan responded: "OK – Let's go ahead. Call Cindy."

A complete feeling of peace burst like a flood throughout our home. Without delay, I said goodbye, pressed the button to hang up, then let the button loose and punched in Cindy's number. Thomas saw my smiles and excited voice and smiled at his talkative and obviously-joyful mommy.

"Cindy, Jonathan and I absolutely know that this is the baby that will make our family complete." It felt so good to say those words!

"Wonderful! We'll send you the documents for the Arkhangelsk Region." Cindy paused. "But I need to warn you: There's always a possibility of losing a referral. If any of the child's relatives were to visit her during the time of your paperwork and process, then she would be unavailable for adoption."

Cindy's words blew into my chest like frigid wind. I knew she was trying to be realistic, but the blast pressed hard against me.

No, I fought back. *I need to stay positive. I vow to stay positive!*

Hanging up the phone, I clung to the hope and trust that God would guide us and bring our little baby – our little Alexandria – home to us.

I turned to Thomas. "Let's go, buddy."

"Where?" he chirped.

"To the Ash Wednesday Service."

We picked up Michael from school and drove to the church, the boys twittering back and forth about their new baby sister. Not knowing how to express such full feelings, I drove in silence.

When we arrived at the church, the service had already started. The boys and I tiptoed in and, though we normally sat up front, slid unnoticed into the very back pew. The boys settled in, and my eyes pulled in the atmosphere around us. The church's high arched ceiling, blonde wood benches, and ardent red carpet vibrated, but no one else seemed to notice. I wanted to scream out, "We have a baby! We know who she is!" But the service played on in its normal volume and speed. As I let the service sink in, the sounds and people surrounding me pulsed with depth.

Oh, God, here you feel close.

The pastor's words murmured. The boys sat quietly and drew pictures on the bulletin. My mind sang. This seemed the perfect place to be.

God, I'm so grateful. Thank you! Thank you! To you, I'm absolutely and eternally and wonderfully grateful.

No one and nothing could stand in our way now.

Chapter Fourteen

In Angels' Arms

April 11, 1999. My dearest little baby,

Mommy loves you so much. I think of you every moment. How I long to wrap my arms around you, smell your hair, and gaze into your eyes for hours. I want to tell you, "Ya looblu tibia" – I love you – in your beautiful Russian language, so the sound rests gently on your ears. You are a special gift from God. I know we will be a complete family very soon.

But it seems like that day will never be here. I yearn for that day! I so look forward to caring for you. I imagine our time together so clearly: sitting on the edge of my bed, brushing your hair. I see us together in the morning; I'm standing with you, helping you pick out clothes for the day as you peer intently, purse your lips, and cock your head from side to side to choose this shirt over that one. I feel my forearms pushing you back and forth, back and forth, on the swing. And when we go camping as a family, while the boys and daddy are off doing their "men things," I feel you sitting next to me, leaning into my side, reading a book and together feeling the warm sun on our necks.

You will be my daughter in every single way.

I want to find the delicate balance of weaving your Russian heritage into your American culture. You will always have feelings for Russia in your heart. That's so good.

I know that someday you'll have questions for me about your homeland. For some of your questions, I won't have answers. When I think of you asking about your birth family, I hurt. I know that there will be an empty place in your heart, longing for some thread of knowledge of your birth family. I realize that when it comes to your birth mother and father, there's information we'll never know. Maybe there's a plan in that. Maybe there are some things that only God will know, because he's protecting us – and you. I just don't know. We're asking our caseworker to find out every detail they can about your birth family. I want to have answers for you. But I know that's not realistic. For so much of your past, I won't know a thing. I'm so sorry.

This I do know: God knew exactly what He was doing when He created you and placed you in your birth mother's body. He knew you'd come to be our daughter.

Someday, we can return to your country of birth together. Would you like that?

My little one, I am already so in love with you.

Ecclesiastes 3:1 says, "Everything on earth has its own time and its own season." This is our season to wait. In time, you will be with us. I want to be with you right now, this very second. But I know that God holds you in His hands. He knows what's best for us. It's in His time.

I will wait on the Lord.

April 16, 1999. My dearest little daughter,

The days creep so slowly. I want to find you and bring you home.

I had a dream last night. In the dream, for the very first time, we were all at church together. It felt so wonderful. With smiles and laughter, everyone gathered around to meet you and love you. Sometimes it seems the dream will never be reality.

Your brothers look forward to having you home. I overheard Michael and Thomas discussing which one of them would give you your bottle and which one would rock you to sleep. In our own ways, we're all thinking of you.

Yes, my precious little daughter, you are so loved. I wish you could know that, this very minute.

Hear me, God. Hear me, oh my Father. Send your angels to Arkhangelsk, the City of Angels, to be with my little child this very moment, this very night. Let their wings brush peace over her eyelashes. Let their arms cradle my precious baby. Let their protection fall in a blanket over her thin body as she lays in her crib, alone.

April 18, 1999.

Journal, I'm feeling so awful today – like I'm never going to get through this day. I want life to be "normal," but life is so not normal. My waking and sleeping is not "normal." My daily motions are the same, but my heart is not "normal." My heart longs for my baby.

Jonathan is so calm. I don't think he understands at all. My insides churn in anger at his unknowing ignorance and disconnect to my feelings. Aaargh! I want to THROW something! He keeps saying, "God is in control." Well yes, God IS. And on some days, knowing that fact in my head is enough. But other days, it's NOT. I have all of these emotions . . . . What on EARTH am I supposed to do with all of these EMOTIONS?!

I'm REALLY angry. As I write, I'm realizing there's something that happened that really got to me.

Let me tell you what happened.

Tonight, a gal in town asked about our little Alexandria. This woman wanted to know what kinds of things our baby's doing, at her age. You know, like her "developmental milestones" and activities and all of that. I explained that our baby doesn't do much of anything yet, for many reasons. A bit of it is because she had no toys to play with. But, I told her, most of it is that no one picks her up and cuddles her and stimulates her mind and body.

The woman asked, "Is she retarded?"

Then she just stared, waiting for an answer, like she was asking me about tomorrow's weather. Unbelievable!

Defensiveness raged!

People have absolutely no clue as to the impact of their comments. Insensitive words growl and grasp and gnaw on my insides. We're not talking about a picture of a needy child on a card or a camera panning across a room in a television show. Our daughter is not a distant social program to observe, analyze, and critique. This is our child. From eternity, she was destined to be with us, just as any birth child.

Our adoption is so based on faith. I can't explain it. And I really don't have to. Jonathan, Michael, Thomas, and I are part of God's awesome plan. Our Father does not destroy families; He builds them. Jonathan and I were blessed with two beautiful sons and God moved us to adopt. If God directs us, He will provide all we need. He will remain with us. He will give us what we need to parent our daughter.

April 22, 1999. Journal, it's hard to watch the video. Seeing her image is emotionally confusing, straining.

First, the picture is a hollow shell of redundancy. It's the same footage, over and over. I want to hold a living, breathing, moving child. Staring at the screen, the emptiness of the repetitive image reminds me I'm viewing an impotent vessel, empty.

Yet, when I look back at this little child, there she is looking back at me, looking directly into my eyes. And she's so real. This sounds absolutely crazy. It's a movie. An image. But there's such a strong feeling in my heart for this baby.

Her weight is in my arms; yet I'm physically halfway around the world, so far away, and my arms are empty.

May 3, 1999. Dearest Alexandria,
Today is your 9-month-old birthday. I'm celebrating you! You are my daughter!

Right now, I'm here at home, alone, cuddled in my chair in the living room, writing to you. It's a good place to be. And I don't mind being alone. In fact, Daddy took the boys fishing so I could jot down my thoughts. I'm so full of mixed feelings. Let me tell you what is happening.

We've received the wonderful word: Our papers are now in your region. The judge is looking at them. It won't be long now and we'll be flying off to meet you. I looked into air fares today. Wow – what a shock: $3500.00 per ticket. When it comes time to purchase our two tickets, I pray the cost is not that high. But whatever the cost, we will pay it all – to bring you home. Your brothers often ask when we are leaving them, to go get you. They're anxious. I'm anxious. We're all anxious.

I would be there tomorrow, if I could.

I'm missing you, my daughter. That's strange, isn't it? I've never met you face to face, but I miss you, because you are mine in every way.

Weeks passed. No word from Russia. No date to travel. Absolutely no new information about my little one.

Days walked into June. We had our visa pictures taken. I stumbled across a website that tells the five-day weather forecast for Arkhangelsk.

We talked to the boys about what it would be like when we left, with them living with my mom for the weeks we were gone.

I talked to Cindy and Molly almost daily. We knew by now the judge must have looked over our documents. And no one called to ask for more. That was a good sign.

I went about my business of waking, watching the boys, working in the home, and wishing for the hours to pass.

I wrote each and every night in my Journal. Over and over, the same themes twisted through the scribbles: Impatience, wondering, yearning.

And I prayed for my daughter.

At night, Jonathan and I lay nose to nose in bed.

"Jonathan."

"Yes."

Silence.

"When will it end?"

Jonathan reached under the covers to touch my hand and slid his fingers into mine.

"God is in control." His voice was calm. Warm. Steady.

"Yes. I know He is. I truly know He is." And I felt it.

Jonathan wrapped his arms around me and we fell asleep.

Chapter Fifteen

The Phone Call

That sunny Friday morning, Sarah and I lounged in the shade of the oak in her front yard. Sipping iced tea and enjoying the feel of the already-thick grass between my fingers, I couldn't help but think that God must have ordered this perfect sunny day just for our annual garage sale. Gazing across the tables of scattered oddities, the sound of kids screeching in laughter in the back yard floated up and over the house, tickling the ears of the handful of strangers browsing our collection.

Ah, the joys of June and the first month of summer vacation.

Just then, Michael rounded the corner of Sarah's garage and headed straight for us in an all-out run. Thomas pumped his little legs not too far behind, water pistol squeezing with two hands in rapid-fire squirts at his brother's backside.

"Easy, boys!" I called, wincing as a stream of water almost hit an older woman looking over the table of linens.

Michael made a quick dodge, doubled back, and squirted Thomas in the center of the chest. Without hesitating, Michael dashed back around the corner of the house and Thomas, squealing in delight, followed.

Sarah and I glanced at each other. I could tell we were both thinking it: "Boys." The one-word title described it all.

And the follow-up thought couldn't help but rise and wash over my mind: *I love my boys…and I can't wait for my little girl.*

"Elle?" Sarah cocked her head and looked into the leaves above us with squinty eyes.

"Yes, Sarah?" I looked up too. The sound of the fluttering green leaves sounded like soft applause.

"What if you get the call today, while you're here watching the garage sale?"

I'd called Sarah every day this week to talk about details of the sale, and every conversation ended with wondering about "The Call." Every day I awoke to the wondering of whether that particular day would be *the* day.

"The Call" is the moment all adoptive parents wait for; it's the final word: "Come and get your child." It's the moment contractions begin, when labor finally starts, and momentum gains speed. From the moment of "The Call," the intensity rises with a strong sense of, "This is it. No going back. The baby's just about here."

So, in this way, I waited for "labor" to begin. And I was ready.

"Don't worry, Sarah. I emailed Cindy yesterday and gave her your number. She can call me here." I smiled. At this point in the game, I knew to look ahead and cover all the details.

Just then, the phone rang. Its sound penetrated the screen door, flew through the inside of the garage, and blared across sunlight and into our shade. We both jumped.

Sarah sprang to her feet to jog past the tables. I leaned forward to hear the screen door bang. My heart beat thick thumps in my chest.

The door banged again and Sarah stepped from the shady garage into the bright sunlight. Sitting up straight, I searched her face.

"Nope. Not 'The Call' – It was a telemarketer." I let out a nervous little laugh and felt my shoulders drop, smiling weakly at my silly anxiousness.

Throughout the morning and into the afternoon, that phone must have rung two dozen times. Well, maybe seven or eight. But it seemed like two dozen. We carried the phone with us, and each and every time it rang, my heart did that same old silly thumping-in-my-chest thing. By the time our sale "closed" at four-thirty in the afternoon, I felt drained.

Saturday morning warmed yellow as the day before. Mid-morning, Sarah and I found ourselves parked at the same spot on the grass under the oak. This time, the boys played with toy trucks at the side of the drive. Originally placed in a bin for sale, Michael and Thomas had pulled the toys out for one last drive, as if to say their final goodbyes to their shared imaginations with those particular trucks.

I didn't jump at the phone calls today. It was Saturday. No one would be in the office at the agency. I knew I had until Monday to feel the anxiety of waiting for "The Call" again.

When the phone rang, Sarah meandered up from her post next to me on the grass and threw her words over her shoulder. "Just a sec. Let me grab the phone; it's on the card table."

She stepped up to the table and picked up the phone. "Hello?"

Sarah's eyes turned to saucers and a strange smile rose to her mouth. "Just a minute, please." Sarah waved me over, that quirky smile still stuck on her face.

Oh, come on, Sarah. You can't fool me. It's Saturday. I pulled myself up and strolled over with a sigh.

"Oh, stop teasing," I muttered, taking the phone and rolling my eyes.

"Hello?"

"Hi Elle. It's Cindy. I have great news." My stomach dropped to the cement drive.

"July 7th is your court date. You'll need to leave the states about five days before that, and you should plan on being there until about the 14th..."

As Cindy chattered off detail after detail, a small group of customers clustered around the card table, garage sale items in one hand and dollar bills waving in the breeze in the other. Neither one of us noticed. Oblivious, I drank in every single word and tone of Cindy's words, Sarah's ear leaning toward my head, trying to hear. I found myself staring at the card table, its blue hue became more dramatic, the brownish patches of rust dotting the table's edges throbbing rich in color.

Breaking from her stunned state, Sarah noticed the customers getting irritated at the fact that they were being ignored. Sarah started to move.

As she handled the customers one by one, words bubbled over the excited news, and the cluster became alive with shared excitement. I stuck a finger in my open ear to block the chatter and turned sideways to hear Cindy better; noticing, the gaggle of customers shushed their animated exclamations to excited whispers.

"Uh-huh. OK. Yes. We'll do that. Thank you, Cindy, oh *thank you!*" I hung up the phone and Sarah threw her arms around me as we jumped up and down, screaming in joy.

Surprised by the outburst, Michael and Thomas ran over. Michael reached his little hand out to my arm, and Thomas tugged on my shorts. I turned my face down to them and burst out, "Michael – Thomas – We have a court date! Mom and dad are going to be able to go and get your little sister!"

Michael grabbed my waist and yelled out, "Oh Mommy! I am *so happy!*" Thomas grabbed my legs and squeezed; it was a wonder I didn't fall over right there in front of everybody.

June 24, 1999

Dearest Journal,

AWESOME! We're going to get our daughter! The phone call came while at the garage sale today – so totally unexpected! After leaving Sarah's, I spent hours on the phone, making flight arrangements; the boys played in the sprinkler in the front yard, while I tried to find the best flights on the best days. We leave for Russia on July 2nd and hope to return on the 14th. Praise GOD!

Jonathan and I have decided to go to Russia two days earlier than we actually have to be there. The other day, we found out that we have to be in Arkhangelsk on a Monday – so why not spend the weekend before in St. Petersburg? We both agree: It's a good idea to have some time alone, just the two of us.

Journal, there are really three reasons for going early. First, we want to get a sense of Russia, so we can tell Allie one day, when she asks about her home land. Second, I don't think we'll ever have the opportunity to travel to Russia again in our lifetime. St. Petersburg is rich in history – a place of beauty and wonder. I want to see it, feel it, and experience it to the fullest. And third, we want to renew our time together as a married couple before we add another child. Yes, we're a mom and dad. But our love – and even passion – has to be strong together. I have to admit, the exotic city of St. Petersburg creates storybook anticipation. But back to this moment . . .

Oh Journal – Questions spin through my mind: What size clothes do I pack for my baby? She's 11 months old…but how big is she? Does anyone have information on her weight? What kind of food should I pack for her? I wonder – Does she have allergies? Will we be able to find out anything about her family history? Diapers – I can't forget to pack diapers – but how many?

All of a sudden, I feel like a first-time mother again. And all of these thoughts bounce back and forth in my head. I wonder what the weather's like there…Is it warm or cool? We have to take money and carry it on our person somewhere…under our clothes, I suppose…How much extra money should we take with us? Where are we going to carry all that, since it's supposed to all be in cash? Will I be strip searched at the airport?

Speaking of clothes, what should I wear the first time I see her? Oh, what does it matter what I'm wearing?! But what about court… What if the judge doesn't like what I'm wearing? Could that affect our adoption?

Oh my goodness, my thoughts are droplets flung in a million directions. My head aches, I'm easily distracted, and the details of my "to do" list haunt me.

Journal, what do I do?

Focus. Don't focus too much on the future. Focus on the now.

We're in the countdown. From here on out, time's going to fly forward. I can do this.

Chapter Sixteen

Preparing to Leave

June 28, 1999
Dear Journal,
  It's three days before departure.
  Oh, my hours are incredibly busy – gathering the boys' gear for grandma's house, packing our suitcases, getting the documents ready for the American Embassy in Moscow for Alexandria's exit visa. It helped when Molly came over; together we packed a few outfits for Allie, court clothes, camera, film, and baby items. She reminded me to pack light, with few changes of clothing and shoes. It's so nice to have someone who has "gone before."
  I think the boys are ready for their stay with Mom in Kalamazoo. And I think Mom's ready too. She even planned daily events while the boys are there. Knowing Michael and Thomas are with Mom makes it so much easier to leave. But I've never gone away without my boys.
  This feels so strange.
  I'm sure that Michael and Thomas feel my apprehension. They follow me from room to room. I think they're nervous about us leaving; at the same time, I feel excitement in their every move. Right now, I hear them in the other room talking together about "bringing the baby home."
  Oh, my baby. I yearn for you, Allie! I'm amazed how God has already placed a connection between us. I feel you as my daughter. This whole adoption process is remarkable; it's incredible how God works. I want you

to grow up feeling as much a part of us as we feel a part of you. Never doubt our love for you.

I'm in awe that God brought you to us, creating our little girl through another woman's body.

I am forever grateful.

The days fell away quickly; Cindy called us each morning with more information.

"Your Russian facilitator will be at the airport in St. Petersburg to greet you. I don't know his name. But he'll let you know who he is. He will take you to a hotel. He speaks fluent English, and he'll guide you through the steps to complete the adoption. He'll tell you when to pay someone for his or her services and he'll help you exchange your dollars for Rubles."

Each and every phone call, so much information flew out of the phone, it was as if the words flocked, gathering in anxious anticipation before the final take-off to fly south. I ended up jotting these twittering words and phrases on pieces of scrap paper. And those pieces ended up scattered on the counter and in my pocket and on the table, making it harder to capture them all within the net of my mind.

My daily mantra: *Focus. Focus.*

At lunch time, before dinner, and at bedtime, Jonathan and I skimmed the "advised reading material" on travel safety, culture shock, manners, and other oddities that "just might happen" while in Russia. I felt gratitude rise again for the completeness of our agency's "information packet." Words that held a bit of interest before now became documents of utmost importance.

Jonathan booked time off work; I booked the $1500 plane tickets. We laid out our passports, 11-months worth of copies of documents, and phone numbers for agency facilitators. I couldn't help but think, *if the facilitator doesn't show up, how will we know how to dial this guy?* Too late to worry about that now; we'd figure it out. Oh, this was going to be an adventure.

Like a deck of cards shuffled into moving hands, everything fell into place – except for one thing: our visas. They hadn't arrived.

Hours ticked. Another day dragged by. Still no visas. I tried not to panic.

Instead, I became super-focused on making sure everything – and I mean *everything* – was in order, checked and ready to go.

I checked the suitcases. And I checked them again. Looking at the list, my hands lifted and touched each item. Once in Russia, there would be no opportunity to run to the corner store to pick up a forgotten item.

I checked the documents. And I checked them again. One by one, I picked up a document from a pile on the left, made sure it was in order, and placed it into a new pile on the right, marking off each document yet again on my sheet. Once we boarded the plane, there would be no turning back. One missed document meant not bringing home our baby.

The boys kept underfoot, asking questions. Jonathan and I spoke in short bursts of words. Every hour seemed to stretch. And I tried not to think about the visas.

The day before our departure, just after noon, the visas arrived in the mail. Relief rained down on us all.

The tone of our home, though still tense, changed. Jonathan moved in and about in steady rhythm, making sure the house was set to be left alone for the days we were gone. I flitted around with energy, picking up dishes and putting toys away. I put dinner in the oven, realizing I wouldn't have to cook for a couple of weeks. That actually felt kind of good. And shortly thereafter, Mom's car pulled into the driveway.

"Grandma's here!" I called out to Michael and Thomas. With rapid pattering of feet, the boys ran down the hallway in greeting.

Mom barely stepped in with one foot when Michael burst out, "Grandma! I packed my clothes and toothbrush and I have my pillow and of course I have my swimsuit…"

"Me too!" interrupted Thomas, echoing, "And I have my clothes and toothbrush and pillow and swimsuit!"

"Good, good!" Mom picked up their words and hugs, and her voice smiled.

"The outdoor pool might be a little cool yet, but the indoor pool will certainly be ready for us. Tomorrow morning, we'll load bags in the back of my car."

The boys hung on Mom's arms, smiling. Then Jonathan called, and off they went in a burst of movement. With obvious pleasure, Mom watched them run back down the hallway.

"It's finally my turn…Hi Mom." She and I smiled and hugged. She felt so good, and she smelled like fresh flowers.

I helped Mom with her small bag for staying the night, and we chatted a bit. Then we moved to the kitchen and set the table together.

Oh, it was so good to be with Mom.

After dinner, Jonathan and I tucked the boys in bed without much fuss. I think emotional exhaustion softly fell on their little bodies like a blanket. Then Jonathan moved off to finish closing up the house.

I'd just plopped down on the couch after washing and putting away the dishes, and Mom strolled into the living room. It wasn't quite dark yet, but it would be soon.

"You have everything ready to go for tomorrow?" Mom asked.

"I think so," I answered.

We both sat on the couch.

"And Mom, are you ready for the two-week challenge ahead?" I asked back.

"Yes, I'm ready."

Mom looked at the stripes of light falling across the floor at our feet. Her gaze followed the pattern up to the window and into the leaves outside, where the setting sun peeked through. There, her eyes closed slightly, and her lips parted as if wanting to speak.

"What is it, Mom?" I asked.

I wasn't ready for what came next.

Chapter Seventeen

A Mother's Heart

Mom turned toward me.

"Elle, you know that when you and Jonathan first told me that you were going to adopt, I didn't like the idea. I guess I was afraid that your "perfect" family would somehow change for the worse."

Her voice became more quiet. I realized Mom's long drive time coming today gave her hours to think. Now those thoughts came out in a smooth, flowing stream of ideas and opinions and…well, I wasn't sure I wanted to hear.

"You're lucky to have two healthy boys, Elle. Throughout the last months, I can't help but think, 'Why are Elle and Jonathan doing this? Everything is fine. Why would they want to change it all?'"

Mom's voice stopped, eyes squinting with a little frown through her eyebrows, as if trying to squeeze her thoughts through a keyhole. I sat still, waiting, searching the lines of Mom's face. Somehow, months ago, I knew she'd felt this way, but those thoughts – those words in her head – remained unspoken.

Until now.

"I mean, you know. The risk of adopting a baby with "unknowns." Like health issues….In particular, there are serious problems like Fetal Alcohol Syndrome, you know. How do we know that this baby doesn't have something really serious going on?"

Mom's words tumbled, rising in pitch a little bit uncomfortably at the end. I dared not speak. Or think. My tongue felt dry. I nodded one little nod as she continued.

"*You* know – more than anyone – about my struggles during the years I spent as a special ed teacher. I experienced first-hand how hard it can be to work with a child with learning difficulties. I've had to deal with these kids' emotional challenges. It's not easy. I think you know that. Well, since you started this whole adoption thing, all I could think about was, 'What if this baby has problems? Then what? And how is that going to affect Michael and Thomas – and you and Jonathan?'"

The churning river of thoughts stopped, and Mom looked at the cushion between us in silence. Even though she wasn't looking at me, I nodded again, swallowing hard. Mixed emotions drummed ragged syncopations in my head, their sharpness bouncing off the hard walls of the living room.

Why is she saying this? I made myself push away the throbbing, sit still, listen, and not react. I had to.

Still looking at the cushion, Mom continued, "It didn't make sense to me, your adding another child. It costs a lot to raise a child. College education isn't cheap. Wouldn't it be easier to just support a child with one of those programs – you know, send money or something? I have to tell you: These are all of the thoughts that kept going through my mind."

Mom, you don't understand…

"But then I realized," Mom interrupted my thoughts, "'Well, they have to do what they believe.' And I didn't argue too much after that."

Silence returned. I sat quietly. Then I whispered, "I remember."

Those are the only two words I could eek out. I *did* remember Mom looking upset, asking questions, and in the end, not saying much. It was uncomfortable. I guess I pushed it all out of my mind.

It really hurt to have Mom question us. But I guess, at the same time, I understood.

She loves me. She wants the best for me. There's no doubt her concerns originated from her love.

I need to keep that in mind.

Again, Mom's words surged, undulating.

"And then, in the middle of all my thoughts and feelings came the moment when I saw the video. Looking at little Allie, there was no doubt: I wanted you to go and get her. No matter if I was concerned about you and your safety, flying across the ocean….Even if I worried about the two of you in Russia moving about in a strange land…. And even if it meant me staying here watching the boys for two whole weeks. After seeing Allie on that video, I knew I'd do whatever I could to support you."

Mom's eyes rose to mine, her grin weak, then growing wider. Breath fell from her open lips into my name, "Elle."

The thumping in my chest held echoed in the suspended pause.

"I have seen your faith."

Her words swirled and lifted my heartbeats into the air around my head.

"Through the whole adoption process, I've felt your sense of resting in God's direction."

Her words ran their hands over my soul, smoothing the churning. My eyes watered.

"Your adoption journey has been a challenge to my own faith journey. I would like to say I've learned just a little bit more how to step out in faith. I want to put my trust in God – And the struggle has been to know how to balance my reliance on God with choices to do smart things and make intelligent decisions. I guess this experience has been a good way for me to learn how to balance it all."

The room felt completely soft again. I blinked, my eyes a little clearer. "Elle, I realize that this is your time. This is your family. And the bottom line is this: I want you to know that I support you."

Oh Mom. I love you.

"Mom," I replied softly. "I truly do feel a certain peace about the whole event. I fully believe that God led us to this child. She's our daughter."

Mom nodded. The sun now lay below the rim of the earth. We sat there for a moment, feeling still and good.

"And," I added with a faint lilt, "I'm sure you're going to have a good time with the boys."

"Oh, yes. No doubt! We've planned *grand* things!" Mom's words rebounded with energy. The atmosphere took on breezy-ness, as if the first part of our conversation never happened.

Mom continued, "We're going to Binder Park Zoo, and to Kellogg's, and we'll swim at the pool at my apartment, of course....And if they get homesick, I can bring the boys back here to sleep in their own beds." Mom stood, and I followed, slower, measured in my rising. Light and frilly conversation couldn't stay; in a flicker of time, the weight of the moment returned to Mom's demeanor. We hugged a long time.

"Goodnight, Elle."

"Goodnight Mom. And Mom?" I looked straight into her eyes. "Thank you."

"You're welcome."

Before I knew it, morning walked in tall and ready.

There Jonathan and I stood by Mom's car to say goodbye to the threesome. I took in a long, deep breath and held both boys in my arms. They felt so good. They smelled like grass. Tufts of hair tickled my face, catching a tear on my cheek. Then both boys scrambled into the back seat of Mom's car.

They're so young; I can't believe I'm leaving them. When we come back, all will be different. Am I giving something up with them, to be a mother to someone else? What if something happens to us – or them – and this is the last time I see them?

Oh, why do I worry so?

"We'll be fine." As if she knew my thoughts, Mom's words crooned over us in comfort. I looked up to see her eyes, watery and intense. We hugged; both our bodies trembled as tears of joy and anticipation wet our cheeks. Jonathan placed his hand around my shoulder and hugged Mom too.

We stepped away and Mom closed the car door behind her. She started the car and pulled around. Michael and Thomas stuck their arms out the windows as far as they could, with all four hands waving. Loose bits of gravel crunched between the cement and tires and as background to the chorus of "Bye Mom! Bye! Bye Dad! Byyyyye!"

The car rounded the corner and was gone.

An outdoor-quiet hung in the air; the pure and simple notes of a handful of birds mixed with the murmur of rustling green leaves. Arm in arm, Jonathan and I turned and walked into the empty house. Letting go, Jonathan rubbed my arm in a sideways movement as he always did. He smiled and started upstairs, tossing the words over his shoulder, "I'm going to get the bags in the van."

The house felt so quiet and empty. Standing there felt dreamlike, pregnant with all of the effort and anticipation and time leading up to this day. Standing on the brink of leaving, my knees wanted to shake. But I wouldn't let them.

Lord, I prayed. *Give me confidence.*

It was time to go.

Chapter Eighteen

Over the Ocean

Have you ever heard of a "puddle jumper flight"? It's when you board a dinky little airplane that flies you on a short flight from one airport to another. From our little MBS airport to Detroit Metro, that was our flight. We went up, leveled off for a few minutes, and descended. A week before, Cindy told me to leave jewelry home; taxiing into the gate in Detroit, my thumb fiddled absentmindedly on the bare spot on my ring finger where the wedding band used to press. I wasn't sure whether it was the quick-up-and-back-down flight or the apprehension tickling my stomach; either way, everything around me felt unreal and alive and unbelievable.

Off the plane, we scurried to the next gate to board the KLM flight for Amsterdam. Rolling our carry-on luggage past crowded gates, we didn't talk. Jonathan walked at a brisk pace, looking so calm. My hurrying feet made quick click-click noises on the beige tiled flooring. I don't think I looked calm. With the tall ceiling arching above, I felt like a nervous chipmunk scuttling through a busy forest.

Near the gate, coffee smells wafted from center kiosks. A maintenance woman wearing clear plastic gloves wheeled a large, lined rubber garbage can nearby. A couple standing next to us muttered together in a strange language.

People lined up patiently and funneled steadily in and onto the gateway to the flight. We flowed as part of a surging sea of dazed people, moving like Jonathan and the boys' fishing bobbers – in and out, around, and almost bumping, but not....and finally swooshing down the funnel walkway and into the plane.

"You want the window seat?" Jonathan's polite voice sounded muffled in the crowded aircraft. The large lady across the aisle squeezed her body sideways in contortions, trying not to bump us as she hoisted her bag into the rack above.

"No, you go ahead. You can look out the window. Maybe we can switch later. I'm going to read my book first."

The plane took off. I could feel my heartbeat pressing against the back of the seat.

As the plane started to level, I tried to read but found myself skimming across the same sentences over and over. Sticking the book back in my bag, I reached down into the side pocket and pulled my Journal. Holding my favorite floral pen poised, I waited. The engines still climbed, and so did my adrenaline. I couldn't scratch out a single thought.

I closed the Journal and stuck it back.

There I sat, hands flopped together empty on my lap. The seat belt light went off. I watched the team of pretty Dutch stewardesses swish by, their blue eyes flashing along with their bright red-lipped smiles. Back and forth. Back and forth. Before long, I knew each one's blonde hairstyle, the color and style of their earrings, and the color of each one's nail polish.

Time ticked. I tried to sleep. The tallest stewardess brought me an itchy green blanket. I squeezed my eyes shut and snuggled up to Jonathan. The roar of the engines droned on. The cold metal armrest between us poked my ribs. I moved again. Tossing my right leg over my left, my foot hit the seat in front of us with a thump. The balding gentleman in the seat glanced back at me, his glasses falling part way down his nose.

"Sorry..." I half-whispered.

I never could sleep even partially sitting up, and it obviously wasn't going to happen here either.

"Jonathan?"

"Hmm?" He was half asleep. *How could he sleep like that?*

"I need to walk."

"Um-hmm."

Moments became blips. Dashes. Snippets. Like little ribbon pieces all lined up in a timeline that went nowhere : Get up. Walk up to the first class curtain. Turn around. Walk back to the seat. Sit down. Lean out the aisle. Look up the aisle. Look down the aisle. Sit and lean back. Look up. Adjust the air nozzle above. Look forward. Pull the magazine out of the mesh rack. Flip through the magazine. Put the magazine back. Jonathan's breathing slowed, his head tipped a bit, and his eyes closed.

Sigh.

Get up again. Walk to the back. Peek at the stewardess behind the edge of the restroom. Smile. Walk back. Sit down. Cross legs, careful not to bump the seat in front. Look out the window. Can't see a thing. Look at the back of the head of the lady next to the bald man. Uncross legs. Stare. Sigh. Pull Journal out of the side of the carry on. Rustle through purse for my favorite floral pen.

Breathe. Close eyes. Think. Smile. Breathe deeply. Open Journal. Pick up pen.

July 2, 1999
Dear Allie,

Daddy and I are on our way. We've completed one flight of four to our destination of becoming your parents. OK, it was only a 35-minute flight. At least we're that much closer to you, my darling little girl.

Now we're on our way across the ocean.

I'm dreaming about our first meeting. Will you hug me? Will you be shy? From viewing the video over and over, we know your face intimately; yet we're complete and absolute strangers to you. You have no thought to how we've anticipated this day.

In just hours, we'll be in your native land.

It's strange to leave America. It's hard to leave the boys. It's unsettling to leave the comfort of our home and country. We're flying away from everything we know and into something unique and wonderful – your Russia.

I'm truly excited.

Stay safe, my baby. We're on our way.

Jonathan and I fondly called the main dish of our meal "mystery meat." It wasn't too bad. And eating side tracked me for a little while.

I found myself staring at the movie screen, its surface blaring a cartoonish world map. A little red line drew our flight across the Atlantic, and the little animated plane moved closer to our destination. What seemed an eternity of hours later, I finally felt the belly of the plane lower; we began to descend.

I pulled out a stick of chewing gum, popped it into my mouth, and double-checked the Journal. Yes, it rested snug and deep in the bag.

During our three hour layover in Amsterdam, we walked up and down the terminal, in and out of almost every store. We bought over a dozen large European chocolate bars for gifts. Sitting on a bench, I ate one. Enjoying its creamy dark richness, I fiddled with the wrapper, cocking my head at the picture of the funny little man and strangely-lettered words.

"Mmm. Jonathan, you should have some of this. This is wonderful."

"OK. If I absolutely *have* to," he teased, a smile peeking out from beneath his dark beard. I handed him the last piece and swallowed my last bit. Then I stuck the wrapper in my purse for Allie's memory book.

We got up again and wandered a bit more throughout the clean, modern airport. It felt good to stretch my legs.

"Hey, honey," Jonathan nodded forward. "There's a computer station just ahead."

I followed his gaze. Sure enough, Jonathan's nose sniffed out technology.

"You mind if I email the guys at work?"

I smiled. "Oh, no. Go right ahead. I'm going across the aisle to that little shop with the cute little ceramic windmills." His computer terminal couldn't hold a candle to those adorable miniature wooden shoes and rows of chocolate bars.

Some time later, Jonathan wandered in. "It's time to get to our gate." Sure enough, just when we got there, the man behind the counter called to board the flight.

This time, I sat by the window. As the plane left the ground, I peered at the passengers, wondering why they traveled. Most of the men and women wore conservative clothing, quite plain. And most spoke in thick-sounding words, some in Russian.

I wondered, *do we look American?*

In between the two movies and snack, I continued to people-watch. The never-ending engine droned its back drop. Eventually, my eyes grew heavy, and I fell into a numb slumber.

Ouch!

A sharp, piercing pain bit my ear drum, waking me with a jerk.

We're descending.

Jonathan stirred; sitting, he wrenched his neck to peer out the window at the thick grayness.

We must be in clouds.

Rummaging in my purse, I grabbed gum, peeled it out of the wrapper, and chomped down hard. Squeezing my jaw tightly together then opening again, I forced a yawn. Finally, the pain ebbed.

"Seatbelt, please." The stewardess pointed to my lap. I clicked the belt on and glanced at Jonathan. His eyes stepped aside for a moment to peer into mine and smile. I grinned back; he pointed, and I looked out the window. We'd cleared the clouds. There, below, the dark land of Russia stretched before us. Our eyes met. My skin prickled.

The nose of the plane angled downward. The engine's roar increased. And while the plane's belly pressed downward, the top of the city of St. Petersburg grew.

Plane wheels scraped the runway. I turned to Jonathan. He squeezed my hand.

Russia. Finally. We're here.

We're coming, Allie.

Chapter Nineteen

Welcome in St. Petersburg

"Do you think he's here?" My forehead wrinkled with tension. We'd walked off the plane in St. Petersburg very close to each other. The dimly-lit fold-out hallway spilled us into the airport, pouring the feeling of "lost" over my head, soaking fear into my frame. The cluster of moving bodies blended with pressing sounds of the Russian language. People shuffled in one direction, brushing our sleeves. We clenched our bags tightly and held arms. The people around us looked so sure of where they headed.

"Let's keep walking," Jonathan said, voice low.

Faces crowded about as we walked. Light fell dimly, not in clean, well-lit shafts of light like in the American or even the Amsterdam airport. Dark shadows hid near walls; musty smells mingled with body odor. Because of the shuffling wall of moving people, the airport seemed small. So many bodies. So many.

"There!" A clean-cut, 30-something gentleman wearing gray dress pants held up a white piece of cardboard with the word, "Conner," printed in large black letters. We ran forward; in happy relief, my hand automatically rose to the man's shoulder, touching his blue button down shirt just for a second. Realizing his stiff, professional stance, my hand fell back to hold my bag.

"Hallo. You are the Conners." The man's statement rang in a strong, thick accent. We nodded. His freshly-shaven face smiled, turning his cheeks to "apples" while his slightly-wavy brown hair stayed combed neatly in place. Unlike most of the men around us, our greeter's showered tidiness offered no smell.

"I am Kirill. Come. We will get your luggage."

We followed Kirill obediently to the luggage carousel. Kirill's body pushed into the crowd, seemingly without care. I looked around and noticed: Most everyone used their body in this way.

Kirill and Jonathan grabbed our bags and we wove through the crowd to the outside of the building. We walked in silence, taking in the strange sounds, sights, and scents.

The air felt heavy. But it wasn't a heaviness of humidity. The only way I can explain it is that it felt like a heaviness of spirit. The sounds of voices hung in low, thick tones. Faces stared in seriousness, eyes stony. Occasionally a voice rose in emotion, but it wasn't the emotion of joy. It was just a stronger emotion of the thickness.

I felt anxious to leave the airport.

Outside, mid-afternoon light fell in grayness. Only a few trees dotted the ground in the distance. A huge parking lot loomed in front of us, filled with small cars.

Strange. I don't see or hear any birds.

Kirill's cream-colored compact car waited in front of us, in the semi-circle right in front of the lot area. Kirill placed a key in the key circle to open the trunk and lifted our bags inside.

I can't believe our bags fit into that little space.

Kirill motioned for Jonathan to sit with him in the front. Jonathan opened my door and I crawled in the back, placing my carry on bag next to my lap. I don't know the model of the car. But it felt old. Like from another decade. The engine puttered to life, and Kirill pulled away from the edge of the road, wheels bumping over rough cement.

Under the noise of the engine, I heard Kirill's voice speak toward Jonathan.

"How was your flight? Did you eat? You like the food?"

Jonathan chatted back, the conversation stilted in bursts of question and answer. I gazed out the window, watching strange buildings and street signs whiz by as our little car bumped and turned sharply. Used to our van, I felt uncomfortable as the worn and tattered interior pressed its cramped closeness against me. It was as if I'd step back into the 70s.

St. Petersburg, "the Venice of the North," now rose before us. We wove through streets and passed the river running through the city, and I marveled at the beautiful detail on the buildings. Each building stood a different color, like a huge garden of buildings. Pastel yellows and pale blues stood hazy, as if a great giant stepped in, wielding a huge paintbrush, stroking a grayish film of dirt over all the beauty. Jonathan leaned back and whispered, "Russia needs a good power washing."

Cars and people moved everywhere. The roads stretched with no or little curb.

"Do you see that statue of the man over there?" Kirill asked. "Do you know who that is?"

Jonathan, my "Jeopardy" TV-show genius, stated with confidence, "That's Peter the Great." Kirill's eyebrows lifted, and he nodded one affirming nod. I don't know what Kirill thought of us, but I do think that at that moment, Jonathan's standing with him rose a notch.

We arrived at the Hotel Oktiabryskia. Just as the agency said he would, Kirill reserved our room days before. The four-story pale-green-painted cement hotel loomed before us. Heavy windows with thick painted sills all stood shut, not a one open in greeting this warm day. Everything about the building looked aged.

Oh my gosh. No trees. No flowers. Come to think of it, I don't think I've seen shrubs or grass either. Everything's cement or brick.

Dorothy, you're not in Kansas any more.

Kirill swung the car to park against the curb and turned off the engine. "This hotel was named after the historical events in the bad fight happening in Russia during the month of October," Kirill informed. I wasn't sure what that all meant, but yes, the name of the hotel sounded like the name of the month.

Kirill must think his job is also that of a tour guide.

We lifted our bags from the trunk, walked up a few steps to the hotel's narrow double doors covered in heavy dark paint, and stepped in. There wasn't much of a lobby. A small gift shop hid in the corner. The entry felt dark and thick. Kirill confidently strode across the strip rug to the registration counter, a chest-high bastion. We followed.

Kirill greeted the woman hiding behind the front desk, and they spoke quick, sharp words in harsh dialogue. I watched her dark bun, a tight bundle of hair pulled sharply behind her face; it bobbed in and out of sight as they sputtered words back and forth. Then she handed him a set of keys. Kirill turned to us.

"The day after tomorrow we fly to Arkhangelsk. You see the city, yes?" Kirill's eyes raised a little as he asked. I had the distinct feeling that it was strange for him to play host for an adoptive couple for more than one day.

"Yes. We planned it that way. We want to see the city, so we can tell our daughter about it when she's older."

Kirill didn't seem to get it. Or maybe he didn't care. Instead of continuing our conversation, our words dissipated down the dark hallway and Kirill asked, "You need dollars exchanged for Rubles and Kopeks?"

We nodded. Kirill led us down the dim hall to an exchange booth. There, a wrinkled old man sat on a metal stool in his caged office. We placed American money into a dish and slid it through a narrow opening under the metal wire. The man grasped our bills and jingled a fist full of Russian money into the dish. Sliding the dish back, Kirill pulled the dish toward himself to count, checking for a fair exchange. It must have been right, because he nodded and handed us the money. We divided the cash between us, placing the small papers into Jonathan's pockets and my purse.

Boy, we sure do have to trust him, don't we?

We followed Kirill up the stairs to our room. Old carpet with deep red and black, swirling designs lined the hallway, soaking up the sounds of our footsteps. We stopped in front of a thick, tall door. Its painted blackness held our faint reflection.

Kirill turned the key, swung open the door, and stepped back to let us into the room. A sitting area touted a golden cloth couch and cheaply-varnished coffee table. Standing beyond were two single beds. My gaze moved to an old television sitting in the corner on another cheap wooden table. Pale wallpaper with flowers covered all four walls, its off-color pastel dim against the whitish lace curtains. Dark black tiles stretched across the floor. A single rug lay quietly in the center of the room.

"Thank you, Kirill."

"Here is my phone number," Kirill answered. "If you need you call me. I will call you tomorrow to tell you what I have arranged for you. Have a good night"

So Kirill was indeed our travel guide.

The door clicked closed. We each flopped onto a bed. Soft from years of use, the mattresses sunk down, settling us into the middle of the blankets. Jonathan kicked off his shoes and stretched, making a tired "oohmph" noise.

We lay there with no words, our bodies emanating lines of tiredness. Within minutes, Jonathan's breathing changed; I knew he'd fallen asleep. I lay there and watched Jonathan for an hour, light coming through the lace sheers on the window, making a pattern on the floor. I dozed, then woke, then dozed, then woke. Thoughts of Allie floated in and out of the realization that the next two days were supposed to be a vacation of sorts. Finally, I couldn't stand it any longer. I sat up on the edge of the bed and looked at Jonathan.

I'm not going to get a chance to be alone with Jonathan for a very long time.

"Jonathan?"

Jonathan stirred.

"Jonathan. Please wake up. OK?"

Jonathan opened his eyes and stretched. He pulled up to sit on the edge of the bed, then stood and stretched again. He blinked. He looked like a rag doll just pulled from a toy box.

"We're here. In Russia. In St. Petersburg. We only have a little time. I'd really like to go out together."

"OK. Sure. Yes, you're right." Jonathan sat back on the bed and blinked; reaching down, he put his shoes back on. With few words between us, we took turns to use the bathroom. I clicked open my suitcase. There on the top sat a wrinkly map of St. Petersburg I'd copied from the back of a Lonely Planet book. Jet lag weighed on my body. I grabbed the book, breathing deeply to wake my mind.

Baby Allie, I'm so anxious to see you. But right now, I'm going to try not to think about you. God took us this far to get you; we'll be with you soon. Now it's mommy and daddy's time.

Jonathan swung open the heavy door. And in a bizarre and dreamlike daze, we stepped out.

Chapter Twenty

Exploring with Zibi

Nevsky Prospect, the main road, stretched before us. Cars hurried by, dashing in reckless speed. We dashed too – across the street to the narrow, cracked sidewalk on the other side. Spectacular buildings with statues rose on either side of the road. These buildings weren't too tall – maybe four stories or so – but oh, how they held the most wonderfully-carved stone curls and details!

We walked now, passing by a store with beautiful cherub faces carved in stone and lined up on top, their two-foot-wide faces smiling in chiseled beauty. My eyes drank in the essence of thick Russian history etched around us. It felt as if I walked through a painting, its vivid colors and strange lines swirling around me.

That afternoon and into the night, we wandered for hours. We passed near the Hermitage Museum where four giant naked white-marbled men stood as pillars holding up the building's porch. And we crossed an arched bridge over the river Neva lined with monuments of men rising nobly on horses. Building after building, street after street we walked, commenting on the exquisiteness with an unmistakable dullness pressing down. It was as if the entire town was draped in a sheer film of dirty gray.

With each step, a new thread of relationship wove into the fabric of our marriage. Or maybe it was an old thread taking up its original place. Whatever its origin, it was good. It was so very good.

But oh, I couldn't *not* think of Allie. Here we walked among her people. We passed old men, aged babushkas, and little boys holding tight to stern fathers' fists. We passed bouncy young girls, beautifully-shaped young women, and stooped old women. In each one of their faces, I searched. I searched to somehow look into the heart of their Russian souls.

My child has an American soul tied in symmetry to her Russian soul.

If Allie somehow stayed in Russia, growing and living here, what would she be like? Would she walk a street, holding the hand of a babushka?

Pushing away the "what ifs," I reached my eyes into the city around me.

We came to a large cement area and found ourselves gazing into the face of a monument of Catherine the Great – her form rising three times our size into the sky, grand gown flowing in frozen dark stone, stern face staring nobly to the horizon. We paused, tired. And we gazed, amazed.

As we stood in silence, a foreign man wearing baggy black shorts walked up. Wiry tufts of silver hair stuck up from his head, and smiling wrinkles danced from the corners of his eyes. He wore a black tank top that looked more like a man's undershirt, an unlikely match to his gray wool socks rolled down to meet the tops of brown walking shoes.

Motioning with his hands, we gathered that the stranger wanted to take our picture in front of the statue. I handed him the camera and we turned away, walking toward the Catherine the Great's base.

"Jonathan?"

"Yes?" Our footsteps fell in rhythm together on the cement.

"We just handed our camera over to a complete stranger. What if he runs off with it?" I wanted to flick my eyes back over my shoulder but didn't.

Jonathan shrugged. "Oh well. Too late now."

"Good!" The stranger yelled out to us in a deep accent. "Stop!"

We turned. There stood the stranger, our camera up to his face, waving his hand up and down – more like he was patting the ground than telling us to stop. We placed our arms around each other. The stranger clicked the button and pulled the camera away to look sideways

Miracle in the City of Angels

at the lens with a squinty eye, and then waved us back to him with a smile.

"Thank you," we smiled, taking back the camera. The stranger nodded and smiled.

"Where are you from?" Jonathan offered.

He smiled and nodded, answering, "Yes."

A flicker of our eyes met, and then Jonathan tried again.

"America," Jonathan said, pointing to his chest and then waving in my direction.

"Ah!" The stranger pointed to himself. "Poland."

He carried a translation dictionary, and with some points and grunts, we found out the stranger was a professor teaching in St. Petersburg for the summer. Neither one of us could pronounce his name, so we ended up calling him "Zibi," which was as close as we could come to his true name. Zibi obviously thought it "cute," letting out a little chuckle the first few times we spoke the nick-name.

We didn't communicate much. He spoke very little English. But there was no mistaking the understanding that he adopted us for the rest of the evening.

Zibi led us to the Cathedral of Our Lady of Kazaan; its six enormous pillars towered to hold the center of the building, the beautiful copper dome covering the heart of the cathedral. A priest's chants echoed while men and women silently filed in, kissed a glass-encased bible, prayed, and walked out.

Then Zibi waved us to follow to The Church of the Resurrected Christ. Nearing the entrance, Zibi motioned for me to take my scarf and cover my head. Glancing, I noticed all the women wearing head coverings, so I did as I was told. We placed a few coins into the gold bowl at the entryway.

Entering, I gasped in awe. Thousands upon thousands of mosaic pieces met in dazzling splendor, placed into murals showing the birth of Christ through his death and resurrection. I vowed to hold Allie's culture in high esteem.

We shuffled to the side to let our eyes wander. I wanted to feel the beauty sink into my skin before taking another step. Then we shuffled to another area, stopping again to absorb the ambience in quietness. I don't know how long we did this. But it wasn't long enough.

"Elle, it's getting late. I think we should start heading back to the hotel." Jonathan's words echoed in the church. I nodded.

Turning my eyes from the splendid surroundings, I noticed an old woman, just off to the side. On her knees, with a bucket of water beside, she held a rag. And there, on all fours, she pushed the tattered cloth in an aching, slow tempo against the floor. The woman stopped scrubbing to lean back on her heels and dipped the rag in the brownish water. Her face turned in just enough of an angle for me to see the myriad of wrinkles etched sadly into her worn face.

And then I noticed it. On the floor.

A small wooden bowl sat next to her bucket.

A middle aged man walked by. The woman stopped scrubbing. Lifting the wooden bowl, she offered a gentle smile, begging for a coin. The man didn't even drop her a glance.

My heart ached at the dichotomy of the magnificent church and this woman. I wanted to reach out with my arm, lift her to her feet, and take her to the nearest restaurant. Her eyes held a story I longed to hear. Jonathan and Zibi were already moving into the sunlight. I whispered a prayer for the washerwoman and followed the men outside.

We headed in the direction of our hotel. With lingering eyes and neck turned as far as I could, my eyes soaked in the spires of intricacy behind us. Turning to again look forward, I gasped.

There on the edges of the buildings, tucked in the shadows, children slept on the sidewalks. A woman rushed up, hands outstretched, begging, pointing to the little ones. As the mosaic inside, my heart felt broken in a thousand pieces. The mosaic of beauty screamed contrast against the mosaic of human pain.

No one ever begged me for money – or anything – before. I didn't know what to do. Or say.

With weighted hearts, we walked on.

Later, I realized I could have dropped a coin and felt ashamed.

It was hours since our last meal on the plane; neither one of us noticed how much time had passed until now. Sudden pangs gnawed in our stomachs. We entered a Kentucky Fried Chicken and bought a familiar meal. The cost: 88 cents. Then we walked down the street for dessert at Baskin Robbins. How very strange it all felt.

Zibi accompanied us to the hotel. Walking up to the door of our room together, Jonathan reached in his shirt and pulled out a zippered bag hanging from a string on his neck. He unzipped the bag and drew out his money. Offering bills to Zibi, the once-stranger-now-friend waved the bills away with a shake of the head and smile.

"Dasvedanya," we echoed. Zibi smiled one last smile, turned and walked down the faded red carpet hallway. Our heavy hotel room door clicked shut, never to see Zibi again.

Chapter Twenty-One

The Royal City

July is the time for the White Nights, where the middle of the night is no darker than dusk. Romance fell over the city. We stood at the window, looking out at the eerie but beautiful blend of sky and building illumination.

Jonathan came up behind and placed his arms around me. The painted-shut windows brought velvety silence to the room.

"Jonathan?"

"Yes?"

"Do you realize this is the first time we've been alone since becoming parents?"

We stood quietly.

Then Jonathan stepped aside. Reaching to the base of the window, he pried the sticky base open. Fresh air blew gently through the slit. The laughing and shouting of a celebration below drifted in. Jonathan pushed the two single beds together, and we celebrated the moment.

In the middle of the night, mosquitoes slipped in through the slit. We swatted, tossed, and turned. Finally, sleep pulled us in.

The next morning, we awoke to the sounds of pigeon-like birds cooing on the outside edge of the window. I lay for a moment in the intense thickness, pressed by tiredness to the bed. Then, with a push through the weight of jet lag, I walked to the bath to wash.

Turning the knob to let the water flow, yellowish-brown water poured from the faucet. I let the water run. One minute passed. Then two. Then five. But the water never cleared.

I decided not to bathe that day. Instead, I opened the plastic wrapping around the new baby wipes box.

This will do.

And Kirill called on the telephone as he'd promised.

"I have arranged a tour guide. Her name is Oksana. She will meet you in the lobby at 10:00 AM."

We packed our bags. After our sight seeing, we would travel to the airport, so we had to have everything ready to go.

Yes, the day would end in Arkhangelsk.

Oksana's slender 20-year-old beauty lit up the lobby. Her driver, a middle-aged man who never smiled, must have been fighting an upper respiratory infection. He coughed constantly.

Loading the bags, we climbed into the car.

"Oksana – Tell me," I began. "Why are all the drivers men?"

"Oh yes," she answered. "It is because of the danger. When a car breaks down along the side of the road, we do not have ….Mmmm," she hesitated, trying to find the right word. "…Repair shops. And people do not have the money to fix the cars. So it is not safe. The men must drive."

I nodded. *Scary.*

The driver stared at the road and drove. And time accelerated.

Words can't tell you how magnificent the day unfolded. The shapes of letters on the page can't describe the fascinating textures of sound and visual beauty in the places we saw.

Palace Square. The Winter Palace of the Romonov family. The statue of Peter the Great called "The Bronze Horseman." Statues of the Czars. The "Angel on the Square."

Hundreds of years of brilliant history surrounded me. My imagination whirled me away to horse-drawn carriages bringing guests to the Royal Ball.

Among the sightseeing, we stopped to buy gifts: A traditional Russian smock dress for Allie from a quaint clothing store. Hockey jerseys for the boys from street vendors. Matryoshkas, the nesting dolls, for our parents. Hand-carved wooden toys and black-lacquered boxes for nieces and nephews.

Compared to American prices, the cost of each of these items was inexpensive. But for a Russian, the cost was high and excessive. Oksana must have thought we were millionaires.

The morning turned to afternoon. Throughout the day, the culture felt alive, breathing. But now, with the culture pressing around me and burning into my senses, the burning in my heart returned. The familiar aching desire for Allie rushed over me.

My baby, I'm so ready to see you.

Oksana's voice, barely audible over the road noise, half-shouted to the back seat, "Before returning, we must visit one more place."

St. Isaac Cathedral. The tall church held thousands of thin, metal-like stairs curling around the outside of the structure. So many stairs.

And we walked up those stairs. And walked. And walked. My legs ached and heart pounded while Oksana skipped lightly up the steps ahead of us. My mouth went dry, beads of sweat formed beneath the edge of my hair, and I sat down on a thin step to catch my breath.

"You okay, hun?" Jonathan asked.

"I think so. But can you see my heart beating through my shirt?"

Dropping my head between my knees, cool wind blew on my face, and I sucked in air. I stayed there, letting the blood rush back into my upper body.

"Elle. Look." Jonathan's voice brought my gaze up again.

Lifting my head, the view of the expanse of St. Petersburg stretched out before me. *How stunning.*

I drank it in.

Allie, your home land is gorgeous. You will come back and see it some day. I know you will.

Jonathan followed my gaze in a slow panoramic pace. The wind blew my hair. It was one of those moments from a movie.

"It is time to go."

As if on cue from a cinematic director, Oksana's pronouncement rang in perfect timing, sounding oh-so-sweet to my ears.

Time to go to Arkhangelsk.

Time to see my baby.

Chapter Twenty-Two

Into the City of Angels

Back at the St. Petersburg airport once again, the atmosphere pressed around us in anxious motion. Kirill checked our baggage and led us to a counter in the terminal. Then, with a brusque and professional farewell, he was gone.

Like water around my neck swirling higher and faster, fear rose in me. Jonathan and I sat on plastic brown chairs in the waiting area, carry-ons tucked and pressed between our knees. Announcements blared over the overhead speaker, a jumble of Russian language rising and falling in sensations of seasickness. Clueless to the meaning of the words swimming around us, we sat quietly. The hard chair pressed like the knuckles of a fist into my back. I had to speak.

"Jonathan?"

"Yes?"

"How will we know when our flight is announced?"

Russian words rolled out the speaker again. Jonathan twisted his mouth to the side, biting his lip.

"Well." He paused. "I'm not quite sure."

Just then, a gentleman with a pressed shirt sitting in the chair behind us leaned over.

"Excuse me for interrupting."

We both turned. The man's thick accent carved distinct edges onto his English, but the words were clear, strong, and with a southern accent.

"I do not want to be rude. But I overhear your concern. They announce your flight is boarding."

Jonathan and I scurried to pull our bags out from beneath us, gathering everything quickly as if the fat drops of an incoming rainstorm were falling with a flurry on our picnic.

"Thank you!" I blurted.

"Yes, thank you," added Jonathan, his quick, single nod giving away inner anxiety in a way that only I could tell.

"Here. This is my flight also. I walk with you, and I will show you." The Russian man waited patiently as we loaded up our arms and, within seconds, we were following him and a small crowd of men and women, through a long corridor to an outdoor parking lot.

"I work with a company in America. My company is based in Texas –"

Ha! I knew it! The southern accent...

"– and I am happy to help you."

"Thank you so much," said Jonathan.

The outdoor air smelled of bitter exhaust. The parking lot opened up to an area with partial bodies of planes strewn in twisted parts, dumped sideways, crippled. As we walked through the center of the dead plane graveyard, rising waters of fear rippled under my chin again.

"No problem," the Russian man continued. "I travel much. I understand your situation." He moved forward with not a blink of concern for the carnage around us.

The air felt thick and humid. We passed the last broken shell of aircraft and approached a full-bodied plane. The crowd pressed randomly to the bottom of the steps, bumping my arms. I noticed everyone around me was male. There were no women. No children. No families.

Then the man who had helped us was gone, pressed somewhere into a corner of the crowd. With my carry-on brushing bodies, I struggled to reach out and hold the rail to go up the steps; Jonathan leaned forward from behind to steady me, and we toiled up the creaking metal.

Miracle in the City of Angels

The inside of the aircraft smelled of smoke and stale air. We found our seats and sat quietly. I grasped Jonathan's hand and gripped. No one offered a smile or kind greeting. Each person's stern face ignored the other. Watching the lack of interaction around me, it felt as if people could not see each other. Each moved and stared past each face and body as if they were the only person on the plane. Fear rose around my mouth and nose now, threatening my ability to breathe.

Dear God, please steady me. Reassure me. Why is this plane sitting here, near that graveyard we just walked through? Did they just replace a part of this plane? Oh God, please keep us safe! We need to make it to our precious child.

The engines roared and the plane pulled itself into the air, making my seat rock. Knowing the seat wasn't supposed to move, drips of moisture swept across my palms. I looked across the aisle. A group of men with stiff-necked collars sat smoking cigars, looking a whole lot like Mafia. One man turned; the intenseness of his stare through slit eyes pierced into my chest. I quickly looked up and away to the ceiling; there, layers of duct tape crisscrossed in pseudo-support. I squeezed my eyes shut.

God, please be with me.

I opened my eyes to look at Jonathan. His eyes were closed as mine had been. I closed my eyes again; my seat rocked and the plane roared.

Time vibrated with the metal sides of the plane; Jonathan and I didn't speak. Hardly anyone spoke. The overly-made-up stewardess walked by and offered a plastic smile but never spoke. And she never offered food or drink. The inside of the plane felt like the basement of an old house that no one had entered in a very long time.

The plane began its descent.

Thank you, God.

The gray day kept us from seeing the ground until we were upon it. Then suddenly, the ground of Arkhangelsk met the wheels with screeching and scraping.

Thank you, thank you, God.

Walking the aisle to exit the plane, I tripped on a loose piece of carpeting and stumbled forward toward the door. Fresh air threw itself into my face in relief as I caught balance again. We walked down the rickety metal steps to cement, where a small crowd gathered away and off to the side.

"Look!" I nudged Jonathan. "There! In the crowd over there....Is that Helen?"

My heart leapt away to the distance, where we both stretched our necks forward to see more clearly. Yes, there on the edge of the crowd stood Helen, our translator. I recognized her immediately from the photo at Molly and Rob's.

Though the air held a breeze, Helen's tall blonde hair coiffed perfectly high over her ears, almost hiding the dark roots peeking through. She was beautiful in her own way, with a strong jaw and serious eyes. Her perfectly-lined lips stood accented against the brightly colored scarf tossed around her neck and tucked neatly into her long jacket. The scarf and jacket billowed in unison with her silky black pants. Helen smiled a polite and pleasant smile as we made a beeline to where she stood on the edge of the crowd.

"Hello Helen!" I spoke first, excitement blowing away the fear from the plane. "I'm Elle – this is Jonathan..."

"Yes, yes. Hello. I am Helen. This is the driver, Victor." Helen's hand waved firmly but gently, motioning like an aristocrat toward a small, skinny man in his late 50s with kind wrinkles etched with hardship. Victor looked up and to the side at us and smiled quickly, much like a young boy looking shyly at his date.

"We will go to the orphanage now. I'm going to take you now to see the girl. It will be short."

My heart leaped – "The girl....the girl" – *Helen meant Allie! We were going right that second to the orphanage! Oh my gosh!*

Giddy feelings bubbled up, and Jonathan and I exchanged corny little smiles stuck to our cheeks.

Something happened to my sense of time from the moment those words left Helen's lips; the air fluttered and rippled around me in dreamy vapors.

Men from the airplane unloaded our luggage onto the pavement with scraping clunks; with surprising ease, Victor's little body lifted our bags and headed in choppy steps toward the cars in a distant parking lot. Then somehow we were in the car, driving fast through countryside and into an old, run-down city.

Miracle in the City of Angels

The car bounced down holey roads past lawns not mowed. Past tall grasses beaten down into walking paths. Past people walking and walking everywhere.

We moved past cars driving, all looking the same maroon color in the same 1972 condition. We drove past apartment buildings half finished – that were clearly not going to be finished anytime soon. We moved past shells of buildings with no windows, no lights, with obviously no one living there, with piles of deserted construction all around. Wood lay stacked up by walls. Bricks lay half buried in grasses. And more long grass grew up past the sides of the stacks of building materials.

As we bumped along, every once in a while, Jonathan's head clunked on the ceiling of the car.

Helen babbled to Victor in Russian. And then she turned to us. "How was your trip?"

"Good," I said. I didn't want to get into the Mafia and the duct tape and the roaring engines. It didn't matter. We were here.

"Your geerl. She just came out of the hospital two days ago. She had Chicken Pox and pneumonia."

My heart grabbed my ribs. *Allie's sick? Why didn't someone tell us?*

Then, with a jerk, our car turned up a path-like road – and there we were, facing a cement building rising in a stark square shape from the dirt.

The orphanage.
We're here.

Chapter Twenty-Three

Hello, My Little One

As we stepped from the car onto the dirt, my heart sank. I stared at the "baby home" rising so stark, straight, and silent before us. The building spoke dullness. Its thin bricks stood positioned one by one, side by side, top to bottom, tightly laid — tall and in rows pressing upward to the gray sky in regular intervals. The lines and lines of bricks stretched to press against tall glass windows barred with intricate, prison-like white wrought iron casings.

No birds sang. Only faint sounds of traffic scratched the air. The word "grim" washed over my mind, followed by "ghetto."

We walked toward the entry toward six crumbling cement steps. The steps lay chipped and cracking, edged with gaping holes by the base of the building. A single, flat board lay propped as a "porch" over the landing, held up only by three skinny metal poles spaced far apart.

To the side, a pile of bricks lay skewed and scattered in a heap to the side of the door where a lawn might typically extend. But here, the surface of the ground didn't lie calmly as plush grass. The ground quivered as an argument between dirt clods, scraps of wood, pieces of crumbled bricks, and tufts of scraggly grass.

We followed Helen in single file up the steps. Helen turned the knob of the heavy metal door and pushed.

The weighted door creaked open and a wall of air – intense with the smell of urine, dirt, cabbage, and body odor – pressed into us, a pushy odor like I once smelled at the door of an ill-cared-for nursing home.

In the hallway, directly in front of us, stood a tattered stroller. And in the stroller sat a small boy, alone and crying. The pitiful sound of his voice echoed hollowly in the empty hallway.

Looking farther toward the floor, I gasped. The boy had no legs below the knees.

No one came to him. No one answered his cries. The horror of the scene clutched me. A yearning to pick up this little one washed over my body.

"Jonathan..." I whispered.

"No, Elle. It's not our place," he whispered back. "Let's not do anything to mess up our adoption."

I nodded, my chest heavy, pained. The thick door thudded behind us.

Helen motioned for us to follow her down the hallway. Helen's high heels clicking on the linoleum. I followed down the dim, narrow hallway, with Jonathan close behind. The little boy's cries followed too, fading as we walked farther and farther away.

Choking air, hot and thick with the smell of mildew and urine, pressed into my cheekbones. A strong urge to cover my face pushed against me, but I didn't dare lift my arms to fight back the smell seeping into my nostrils.

I couldn't speak. Rapid heartbeats made my fingertips tingle, and my head felt cottony and thick. The bleak, calloused walls pressed in, desolate and dreary. Dismal, somber nothingness pushed its unwelcoming silence against me.

My baby, my treasure, is here. Oh, Dear Lord....

Helen's heels stopped. We stopped. She turned. "Stay here please." Her thick "r" rolled its echo down the hallway.

Jonathan glanced at me and raised an eyebrow as if to say, "Do we really have a choice?"

Helen stepped through a doorway and was gone. We stood alone. Neither one of us spoke.

Where did she go? Why did she leave us alone?

The stench seemed to be getting worse. I wanted to run. I wanted to breathe fresh air and see my boys.

Jonathan pulled the video camera from the bag slung over his shoulder. I heard the click of the machine as he turned it on. Helen reappeared, followed by a robust woman wearing a white coat – with something – no *someone* – in her arms.

Now time blurred and whirred and spun. The woman in the white coat – the caregiver – stood before me, her black hair pulled back tight into a bun like the woman at the hotel desk, in strong lines against her stony face. She held a baby, body facing outward toward me. The baby rested on one of the caregiver's large hands; the woman's second hand wrapped around the baby's middle.

It was a little girl. She wore fuzzy red pajama-like sleeper pants, a bit worn but still quite crimson, hanging in baggy folds on her tiny body. Over the red pants fell a white knit frock with a crochet design bibbing. A single pink string of yarn dangled in a saggy bow from the edge of the baby's collar.

The baby's arms stuck out as if she were trying to catch herself from a fall. Her legs extended a bit stiffly. And the baby's blue eyes stared in blankness – straight ahead, deep set in puffy, dark circles. Her cheeks sagged, sunken down so the pudginess hung from a gaunt face to rest around pursed, bright-red lips. She had no hair to speak of, just short blonde pieces cropped tight to her head.

Who is this baby?

Helen stepped aside, and the caregiver held out the child to me.

Allie?

I took the baby in and cradled her body in the crook of my arm.

Is this the right baby? She looks nothing like our referral video…

I looked quickly at Jonathan. The lens of the video camera looked back. I looked down at the baby.

This baby is so tiny. So boney. So pale. So unresponsive.

Goopy mucous came from the baby's left eye. With convulsing tightness, the baby coughed a deep, wet cough. I looked into the baby's blank eyes. She looked back. Then I saw it. I saw it in her eyes. The same look as in the referral video.

Allie! There you are! My baby! This is my baby!

A feeling of completeness washed over my entire body.

The caregiver spoke to Helen in Russian. Helen turned to me, brisk voice piercing the air.

"Do you like her? Is she OK? Or do you want another baby?"

Hot, piercing fire leapt into the center of my heart.

Did she really say, "Do you want another baby?!" Oh, Lord God! THIS is my baby! THIS is my daughter! Don't you dare take her away from me! I fought so hard to get HER!

"No, no." I wanted to scream. Instead, the words came out quickly, firmly, falling from my mouth.

"*This* is our baby."

Billows of disbelief continued to fall across my body.

My God, my Father. How could they say such a thing? This is not like picking a box of cereal from the grocery store! This is a human life – a miracle! To "exchange" a life or just "choose another" is unthinkable! Her future would forever be changed…down a dark, murky path of hopelessness. This moment is nothing like I would have thought. But this is my moment – OUR moment.

THIS is my child!

No, this wasn't as I had imagined it. In my dreams, this moment always smelled like sweet baby powder. And in reality – right now – Allie smelled like she hadn't had a bath in days. Her crusty eyes rimmed with redness. Her lungs rattled when she breathed. She hung weakly in my arms.

But none of that mattered. *We are together.*

My arms cradled my treasured little one that I had longed for, ached for, cried for. I began to gently sway and rock my precious baby. My fingers ran down the fuzzy red sleeper bottoms to where her toes should be. Yes, they were there. I felt through the sleeper….

One, two, three, four…. Yes, there are ten. Ten beautiful toes.

I took a quick look over every part of her body, checking out every centimeter, every millimeter. Jonathan reached from behind the camera and touched Allie's fingers. In slow motion movement, Allie wrapped her hand around Jonathan's finger, squeezed it tight into her fist, and pulled his hand to her chest.

Then Allie looked up, into my eyes. Our gaze locked.

Yes! This is me – and this is you! Now I see your little nose and beautiful eyes – the same nose and eyes from the video that I watched again and again and again. Hello, my Allie!

And in that second, I fell deeper in love, deep into Allie's sky-blue eyes. No one else in the room existed.

And Allie smiled.

My baby. My precious baby. My gift. Thank you, my Lord and my God.

I began to speak soft words to my baby, telling her about the outside world. Telling her about her home. Telling her about her brothers and family. She lay mesmerized within the quiet and gentle spirit of love that poured into her soul through my voice.

"Soon, so very soon, my little one, Daddy and I will take you home. Yes, we will. You are ours. And we have wanted you oh, so badly! We have prayed for you since the day you were born. My little one, you will be a happy girl. I promise. You will never be alone again. You will never again lie crying, with no one to hear you and no one to hold you, ever, ever again. You are ours, and we are yours. Forever. We will always love you. We will always be there for you. Always and forever, my sweet baby."

Allie's eyes clung to the sound of my voice. Somewhere in the room a camera bulb flashed. My eyes didn't leave my baby's face. Her body felt warm, tucked into mine.

My beautiful child is finally in my arms.

Chapter Twenty-Four

Settling In

Dear Journal,
 The day came. Today. Finally. We met together.
Like the beautiful sunset that you know is falling onto the horizon, the colors of this magical moment fell into our lives. And this dear and divine moment did not disappoint.

Oh, the shades of our meeting our precious little Allie changed. The seconds together blew like swirling clouds into feelings I could not have imagined. It was a moment so unique and so intense. It was a sunset where each second, the colors changed into more brilliant tones and ambience than the seconds before.

It was a miracle moment.

Journal, at this moment, Truth presses deeply into my soul: Every child is a miracle. Every child is a valued, precious gift. Every life, whether tiny and still within the womb or born into this world, is a marvel, a sensation, an exceptional creation….a gift to a waiting mommy and daddy.

By birth. Or by adoption. It doesn't matter. The miracle is the same.

Allie is our miracle.

But especially in Russia, where the form of birth control is abortion, the fact that Allie was born at all is a miracle.

And Journal, right now, Allie is so sick with infections…and more. At 11 ½ months, she's the size of a three to six month old…her body is long, but her limbs and waist are so skinny! She can't sit up. And her body movements are much, much younger than they should be at this age. It's a miracle she's still here, alive....And with a sparkle in her eye, too!

Arkhangelsk. The City of Angels.

God, you have been faithful. You have given our child angels of protection in this City of Angels. Indeed, the angels have watched over our little one. Our miracle in the City of Angels.

After our greeting in that stinky, dark hallway, Helen motioned us into a small side room that looked a little bit like an office. I sat on the chair to the side; Jonathan stood with the video whirring.

The caregiver talked to Helen, and Helen turned to us to translate.

"The baby might be afraid of Jonathan," said Helen. "She has never seen a man before, much less a man with facial hair."

I glanced at Jonathan, who wasn't daunted by Helen's words.

Then Helen and the caregiver stepped out of the room.

In silence, the three of us enjoyed our first moments together. A different woman entered, appearing to be fixing a typewriter. We barely noticed her there.

My eyes met Jonathan's and he smiled, nodded, and reached out.

I placed Allie into Jonathan's arms.

When Jonathan held her for the first time, Allie looked directly into Jonathan's eyes and smiled. It was if she knew her daddy had finally found her. Jonathan proudly held his precious little girl. His eyes glistened joyously with tears.

Then came a delight.

Allie stretched her petite arm toward Jonathan's beard. Her fingertips gently touched the black whiskers, and her palm fell to cup her tiny hand against his face. It is a tender movement forever etched into my memory.

"I am sorry." Helen stepped into the room. "We have to go now."

Like someone rudely jumping into my calm pool, Helen's abrupt words splashed the moment apart.

"It is soon time for the girl's dinner, and we must go to your home stay."

My heart fell hard and fast to the floor. *So soon!*

Miracle in the City of Angels

Jonathan handed Allie to me in slow and gentle movements. I pulled Allie's little body close. Nestling her head into my neck, I breathed in the essence of my baby girl.

Suspended in the sweetness of the moment, trying to push away the growing twinge in the empty hole my chest, I whispered, "I love you, Alexandria."

The first visit with Allie only lasted 15 minutes. Fifteen beautiful minutes. For 11 months, my arms ached to hold her, and now I had to give her back. I wish I could find the words to describe the awful feeling in my heart at that exact moment. But there is no elegant line of words to write here. There is just one blunt, stiff word: anguish. I felt anguish.

A collection of tears rested on the edge of my eyelashes.

I handed my baby to the caregiver.

Helen, turned to walk away. And we turned and followed.

Oh, I so didn't want to walk away. I wanted to run back and swipe Allie from the caregiver's arms and run outside with her tucked in my arms.

Sensing my anguish, Jonathan wrapped his arm around my shoulder and pulled me in close, and we walked in step. I looked into his eyes. He blinked softly, surely, talking calmness with his eyes. Then he winked a purposeful wink, tender and knowing, and smiled a gentle smile.

Leaning over, he whispered into my ear, "We'll be home soon."

We stepped out into the bright air, and time ebbed and flowed in strange waves. It felt like I was being pushed out to sea on the tide, away from my baby.

Our driver, Victor, rose from his seat in the car to open the back door for me.

"Thank you…mmm…Spaceeba," I nodded to him, adding the Russian word for "thanks." He nodded back, looking once into my eyes and then at the ground.

Helen and Victor took us to an aged and weathered apartment building. This is where we would stay for five days.

"Your host is Igor," spoke Helen. "He is a retired ship worker. His wife is Valentina."

"Igor and Valentina?" I asked, not believing my ears.

"Yes," nodded Helen. Jonathan and I looked at each other, eyes wide, and I shook my head in amazement.

Oh my gosh – Rob and Molly stayed here with Igor and Valentina – two years ago, when they brought home Katie!

Entering from the brightness outside, the apartment building's hallway looked pitch-black. No windows, no lights – just dark cement – and I walked right into a handrail. My breath caught in my throat, and I swallowed against the pain in my thigh, so no one could hear or know.

We walked up a flight of stairs and reached a heavy metal door. Helen knocked and spoke a handful of Russian words in a volume loud enough to penetrate the thick door.

A white-haired man opened the door. His clean-shaven face smiled kindly, in a closed-lip kind of smile that spoke politeness layered with guardedness. He wore a gold shirt tucked into grey pants. He reminded me of an early American photo of the 1800s: stoic, plain, staring straight into the camera with nothing more than a slight grin.

"Heh-low," he spoke, motioning us in with a nod.

"Preeveeyet," I answered and nodded back with a genuine smile. Just knowing Rob and Molly walked in this same place made it all so much easier to breathe right now.

The four of us stepped through the doorway.

Valentina's plump frame stood just inside. Smiling through bright red lipstick, she nodded happily, her auburn hair bouncing. I couldn't believe how much she looked so "cliché Russian," wearing a plain shirt, dark below-the-knee skirt, and thick nylon stockings. Her feet stood wrapped in cloth house slippers, basic and flat.

Helen and Valentina spoke, bobbling words back and forth in the Russian language. Then, following Helen's lead, we removed our shoes. A few small rooms extended out from the living room where we stood. Round rugs dotted the smooth wooden floors. A bedroom. Bath. Kitchen. Guest room.

Simple. Adequate. Tidy.

Helen, Victor, and Valentina walked into the kitchen, leaving us standing with Igor. With pursed and politely-smiling lips, Igor walked to a side table and lifted a large bound book. Motioning for us to sit on the couch, he opened the binding with movements that showed the book was highly treasured.

It was a photo album. Igor slowly turned page after page, showing photos of smiling men and women sitting on this same couch where we now sat. There, with Igor on one side and Valentina on the other, mothers and fathers grinned ear to ear, holding their new little Russian babies. Like a proud grandfather, Igor turned pages, in simple broken English giving faces their names.

Igor knew his valued place in the chain of family-making. And he basked in his "part" in the adoptions of these precious children.

Helen and Victor came back out of the kitchen and headed toward the door.

"I will see you tomorrow morning at 9:00," she said.

And that was that. Helen and Victor smiled, nodded toward us, and left.

Igor spoke few words to us, and Valentina did not speak English. They showed us to our room with a wave and series of encouraging nods. Our bedroom was clean and organized, with a futon bed and a large, black lacquered armoire with two hangers dangling inside.

We rested our suitcases on the floor. And with a wave of her hands that reminded me of the game of Charades, Valentina coaxed us to the kitchen.

While we were looking at the photo album, Valentina must have been busy. There, arranged on the table, laid out in measured array, stood a complete meal for two. Heaping portions of noodles mounded on the plate, and rivers of steam rose from full-to-the-brim bowls of cabbage soup. And again, obeying the wave of her hand, Jonathan and I sat.

Moving about, Valentina waited on us just enough to know that we were settled in. Then, while we ate, she stood in the corner of the kitchen, watching over us like a momma duck watching over her ducklings.

The steaming hot food melted in my mouth, soothing the grumbles in my stomach. As soon as Jonathan took his last bite, Valentina refilled his plate within seconds.

We didn't talk but small talk: "Mmmm, this is good" and "What a nice little apartment" kind of comments. I suppose we felt keenly aware of the need to be good guests.

I felt a little guilty, having her wait on us like that. I didn't know where Igor went. But again, like so many other moments during our time in this strange country, I stopped questioning and just accepted. This was their way.

When we finished and said our thank-you's, Valentina smiled her bright smile and waved us off to our room.

We quietly unpacked and dressed for bed. The futon felt a little thin and bumpy on my back, but I didn't care. My bones pressed into the bed in gratefulness.

We lay side by side, eyes shut but awake, with sleep brushing its feathers against our eyelids. I reached over to Jonathan's hand.

"She's beautiful," I said.

"Yes, she is," Jonathan answered.

"I can't wait to see her again," I said.

"I can't wait to take her home," Jonathan answered.

I smiled. I didn't look, but I bet Jonathan smiled too.

And sleep gently pulled us in.

Chapter Twenty-Five

The Meal

Sleep never slipped into luscious release that night. I moved through the hours floating between asleep and awake, falling down into dreams of home and then coming back up into consciousness as if gasping for air. Like lying on rocks protruding from a sandy beach, the lumpy mattress heightened my fitful washing against the shore of consciousness.

This was not my idea of a vacation.

At the first light, my body ached stiffly, my mind wallowed in thickness, and my skin felt itchy with a sandy irritation that couldn't be brushed away. With Jonathan still sleeping beside me, I reached for my Journal.

OK, Journal; I've had enough. This process has drained life energy from me for months on end. I just want to get my baby, get on that airplane, and walk onto American soil.

I want to be home with my baby.

Scribbling a few groggy words didn't even seem to lift my spirits. I got up, washed my face in cloudy water from the bathroom tap, and dressed for the cloudy day hanging outside the apartment's cloudy glass window.

We'd brought along broad-spectrum antibiotics in powdered form. I made up the medication with bottled water, set it on the corner of the table by the futon, and walked with my cloudy mind into the kitchen for breakfast. There, Jonathan and I ate another polite meal with Valentina watching from her corner.

Igor entered the room. Valentina gibbered in Russian, and Igor nodded his head and looked down at the floor in thoughtful complacency.

We chewed our bread in silence.

I wonder what she's saying.

As if hearing my thoughts, Igor turned. "I go to the store for food now….For today," he said. Nodding one brief bob, he turned toward the door and threw his voice back into the room.

"It is a long walk. When I am back, it is 9:00 and we go to see your little girl."

My heart leapt.

And Igor kept his promise. When Igor returned, Helen showed up right on cue. I barely had time to gather the travel bag stuffed with baby clothes, formula, diapers, water, snacks, and personal items. In a last-second whisk, I grabbed the antibiotic, its weight resting in the palm of my hand a fraction of a second before snugging it into the corner of the bag.

Then we were in the car.

The ride there couldn't go fast enough. The air felt infused with syrup, as if riding in slow motion with the tires sticking into and pulling from the potholes. But arriving at the orphanage, it was suddenly as if we'd never left the place. Walking up the cracked cement steps, swinging the orphanage door open, feeling the pungent, stale air press against my forehead, time erased the last 24 hours. All that existed in my mind was that single and exact moment at hand.

We followed Helen's echoing clop-clop-clop down the dark hallway to a private room at the end. Standing on the dim linoleum floor, a wooden chair and square wooden table took up most of the small space. Off-white lace curtains rimmed its single window, letting in hazy light. Helen motioned for us to enter the room but stayed outside the doorway.

Miracle in the City of Angels

The next moments happened so fast. Each event stacked quickly like blocks, building a thick towering daze in the room's atmosphere. As soon as we turned around and faced the door, a caregiver entered, holding Allie in her arms – again, in a position so that Allie faced outward toward us. Allie's little legs stuck out like a rag doll's. Her body hung, empty of spirit, delicate and uncertain. But beautiful. Oh, so beautiful.

I whispered sideways to Jonathan, "She looks like an Alexandria, doesn't she?"

Jonathan's mouth moved into one of the biggest grins I'd seen yet on our adventure. "Yes. A name fit for a princess."

The caregiver smiled her obligatory smile and lifted Allie out toward me, legs dangling. I reached my aching arms and caught our sweet little girl.

"Hello, little princess Alexandria," I said.

Allie's round eyes, a bit glazed and still rimmed red from illness, moved toward mine in a dazed, searching stare. Then a smile emerged. And it grew, pouring out and melting over her little body. Her arms and legs started moving up and down in happy rhythms, and my heart wrapped around the tempo and danced.

Right away, the caregiver strode out. A thinner woman wearing a white apron and chef's hat entered, carrying a tray into the room. Placing the tray on the table, the woman spoke a handful of Russian at us. Much like I once saw a magician wave the back of his hand over a hat, the woman waved the back of her hand over the food. We nodded, not understanding a single word. And as quickly as she'd entered, the chef-woman smiled the same obligatory half-smile, nodded one up-then-down nod as if trying to move a fly off her nose, and left.

The room felt still. None of us spoke. Allie lay still in my arms and blinked. Then Allie pulled her hand up to her face and watched her slow-motion fingers move one by one. Jonathan and I sat alone in the quietness.

Suddenly, my mind cleared. Jonathan's must have, too, because at the same time, we looked down into the tray.

On the tray sat a huge bowl of mashed potatoes with some kind of chopped meat poured and draped across the top like fudge on a sundae. Next to the Mashed Potato Sundae sat a chipped enamel cup half-filled with dark amber tea. And next to the tea sat a metal spoon – a spoon as big as the one we used for serving dressing and mashed potatoes at Thanksgiving.

"Jonathan?"

"Yeah?"

"This is for Allie, right?"

"I suppose so."

"How do we feed this tiny child with that huge spoon?"

"Mmmm. I don't know."

We kept looking at the tray. I spoke again, words faster this time.

"And she barely holds anything in her hands. Does she even drink from a cup?"

"Hmmm. I don't know that either. This does seem odd."

With each new thought cascading into my head, emotions rose and pricked the insides of my chest, tapping against my ribs in irritation.

"Where's the baby spoon? This is gigantic!"

"Hmmm," said Jonathan.

"Don't they have a bottle filled with milk or formula or something?"

"Mmmm," said Jonathan.

"What about a high chair? Do you think they have a high chair stuck away in a closet somewhere nearby?"

I knew that wasn't so. With each passing second, the mashed potato mound and serving spoon became bigger.

I paused. "Maybe it *is* for us," I said.

Ha! That must be it! But I knew it wasn't.

Jonathan still sat staring at the tray. He lifted his face to look at me. Both eyebrows lifted, and he cocked his head in an, "Oh-well!" topsy-turvy smile and shrugged.

"Honey, I think we're supposed to feed her now. This food. With *this*."

He picked up the spoon and waved it in a little whoop-tee-doo circle like a miniature flag on the Fourth of July.

I knew what he was doing, and I appreciated his humor. But my thoughts just kept tumbling and bashing against my understanding of what is "good" and "right" for a little child. Then an absolutely horrible thought rose in me.

How did they manage to feed all the babies in this home with just a few women on staff? And with this food...with these spoons....There's no way they can feed so many children. At least, not well. They must just shove the food in as fast as possible, to get to everyone....pushing and gagging the adult food down.... And maybe they feed so fast, they get impatient, they must just stop, even when the babies are still hungry, and...

My head started swimming.

"Jonathan?" My voice eeked out of my tight throat. "Will you please feed her?"

Seeing my face, Jonathan nodded and scooped Alexandria's light frame from my arms. As he perched her on his lap, my insides shouted. I got up, reached into the diaper bag, and pulled out an American bib. Tying it around her neck, our eyes met briefly. Jonathan saw the fire of emotion in my eye and didn't flinch. Then all focus fell to little Alexandria.

Jonathan lifted the cup first, gingerly moving it toward Allie's face.

Suddenly Allie's breaths came short and fast. She grabbed the cup with her tiny hands. Drawing the cup toward her open mouth, she slurped and sucked. Most of the tea dripped from her lips down her chin, running noiselessly in dual miniature streams onto the bib. I reached over and dabbed her chin with the bib. Her breaths didn't slow, and her mouth stayed open, waiting.

Then Jonathan grasped the big spoon. Swiping the side of the mashed potato mound with its tip, he meekly offered the too-big spoon toward her dainty mouth. Allie's eyes became spheres. Her mouth stretched too wide and too fast toward the spoon, lips grabbing the mashed potatoes in anxiousness.

I felt dizzy and short of breath.

Oh my Lord, my baby acts as if she's starving. I'm in this beautiful country crushed with poverty – and these babies are the ones hurting, the ones suffering.

Stabbing emotional pain hit the middle of my chest.

I want to be home with my family!

Tears pressed wildly at my eyes. Jonathan kept feeding Allie in calm resolve. All the while, frantic agitation gripped her body. Her eyes did *not* become as almonds again, her breaths did *not* relax. Her neck craned forward like a baby bird.

No, it was more like a starving animal.

"Jonathan, stop."

I couldn't do it any more. I couldn't watch this.

"Let me get the formula that we brought out of the bag."

Jonathan's eyebrows rose. "Are you sure? I don't want to, um, you know, get in trouble or anything."

"She's our baby." Realizing the words burst out a little stronger than I'd intended, I took a breath. I paused. He searched my eyes.

"Almost."

Enough said.

I reached into the diaper bag and pulled out a can of fluid soy formula and bottle. Shaking the can, I popped the top and poured the sweet liquid. Jonathan talked to Allie in little words and sing-song tones. She was obviously still hungry.

"Wait." I reached into the corner of the bag and pulled out the antibiotic. Pulling out a dropper, her first dose slipped into the bottle. *It's time to take back her health and heal the infections robbing her little frame of life.*

I suppose it was a bit bold for us to give her medication. After all, we hadn't been to court yet to legalize anything. But at this point, it was clear that we cared for her more than anyone else on the face of this earth. And in my heart, I was already her mother. I *had* to take care of her.

I don't need a piece of paper to tell me how to mother my sick baby.

I handed the bottle to Jonathan. As he tipped the nipple toward her lips, Allie grabbed the bottle and pulled it in. Sucking hard, the liquid pulsed through her cheeks in frantic draws.

She drained it. The delightful fluid gone, Allie's eyes swept the area, searching for more.

"Jonathan, I don't want to make her sick with too much of something new. I'm going to give her a jar of bananas instead of more formula, OK?"

"Sounds like a good plan," answered Jonathan. As a team, we moved together into familiar territory. I pulled out a jar of baby food and a right-sized baby spoon. Dipping the spoon into the jar, I scooped a right-sized amount of baby food onto its tip. Holding out the spoon to Allie's little mouth, I waited.

Uncertain, Allie awkwardly accepted the baby-sized portion. The moment the creamy food touched her tongue, her eyes opened wide. She turned her head downward to look at the jar of this new, strange pleasure. I scooped again and pushed the little mound into her mouth; right away, she lifted a shaky hand and tried to grasp mine. Unaccustomed to using her arms, her weak muscles trembled with little control. I reached and steadied Allie's arm. Her body shook as she thoroughly enjoyed the delectable new taste.

Don't worry, little one. There's more for you. Much, much more – here, and at home. My princess Alexandria, there are joys and pleasures and peaceful times ahead. No more wanting. No more weakness. You will be strong. You will run and jump and play. And you will laugh a thousand sparkles of laughter.

I promise.

Chapter Twenty-Six

Forward Steps

The next day, our visit with Alexandria took place in an office in the orphanage. It wasn't very private; a Russian woman kept moving in and out of the room, working on an old typewriter. But we didn't care. Anywhere was a good place, and any time was a good time, to be with our daughter again.

When the woman in the white coat came into the room holding Allie (face out, as usual), Allie didn't seem to recognize us. But as soon as we started talking, cooing, and sweet-whispering our love, Allie's face lit up. And then the communication dance began.

We gibbered and jabbered and wrapped her in singing words. She smiled and trembled, waving her limbs involuntarily in joy. Then, as if the joy was too much, Allie looked away, falling into stillness, eyes a little glazed again. We all breathed in, then out, the pause heavy with anticipation. Allie looked back as if to say, "Is this real? Are you still there?" Each time her eyes met ours, the answer was, "yes!" and we gibbered and jabbered again. And with each cadence, with each verse and chorus of this dance, we bonded just a little bit more with our precious baby.

Think about it: We were just placed in a room with our new little child – with absolutely nothing to do – no task to accomplish but to talk to and play with our baby. Oh, such pure moments of focus on each other! Yes, it was very much like the first 24 hours in a hospital room with your newborn.

Making motor noises with his lips, Jonathan lifted Alexandria high into the air over his head. Allie's face lit up with bliss, and she giggled the most beautiful giggles. My heart soared! When Jonathan brought Allie down to eye level, her demeanor changed; she gazed around the room, averting our eyes, curious yet not letting us get emotionally too close. Then, when he lifted her high again, she giggled and laughed and looked at Jonathan's face with such absolute wonder!

In the middle of our laughter and giggles, Helen entered the room with a petite woman.

"This is the doctor," Helen said.

Making restricted gestures, the doctor spoke to us, looking first to Helen, then to us, then back to Helen. Then Helen translated.

"The girl had been placed in a body brace for hip dysplasia. She is doing better and no longer wears the brace. She was very ill with pneumonia and was in the hospital until last week."

My mind screamed. *Why didn't we have this information before coming here? Not that it would have changed anything....But I want to know! This is my baby! Did they think that if we knew, we wouldn't take her home with us?*

Oh, my. The thought sunk in.

That's why they didn't tell us. They didn't think we'd want her. *Oh, my Lord.*

Helen continued. "Do you have any questions for the doctor?"

I didn't. We'd only spent a few hours total within the walls of the orphanage, but I could tell that the staff ran every little minute with strict, regimented measurement. And I was also sure that the schedule was based on caregiver convenience rather than the children's needs. So it didn't make sense to me to ask about Allie's schedule. Soon, for Allie, life would be turned upside down, as we traveled the many hours back to our home in Michigan. Then we'd make a new schedule – a new life.

But I *was* curious about one thing.

"Helen, please ask the doctor about how the baby received her birth name, Anna."

Helen translated, the doctor spoke, and we waited patiently. Allie played with the little bump that was her toe at the bottom of her sleeper foot. Then Helen turned back to us.

"When a baby is born and not given a name by the mother, as in this case," said Helen, "then the delivery doctor chooses the name. Or the baby is automatically given the name of the doctor."

Jonathan and I sat quietly. So our baby was originally named by – or after – a doctor.

To them, so matter-of-fact. To me....So strange.

Allie wiggled in Jonathan's arms in the uncomfortable silence drizzled on the room. I stroked Allie's little arm and Jonathan reached around to hold her fingertips. The doctor looked at us expectantly with a detached stare, neither cold nor hot.

Helen's voice seized the silence. "It is time to leave, but we will return later today to take the girl out for her visa photo."

Goodbye again – so soon! Our time together goes by so fast!

The doctor reached out her hands, and Jonathan began to lift Allie across.

"Wait," I begged. I reached to Allie and stroked her cheek. Allie's eyes turned to look up into mine. As a little smile moved to the corner of her lips, I leaned over and kissed her forehead. She closed her eyes, drinking in the closeness of my body, fluttering her eyelids against the warmth of my breath.

"I'll be back soon, my love," I whispered.

Back in the car with Helen and Victor, Jonathan and I sat quietly. My arms felt empty. The bumps on the road felt hard. I looked through the dirty glass of the half-rolled-window and up into the blue and white painted sky. A comfortable breeze swelled from the origins of the sea, wafting across the cracked walks and dingy buildings, swirling over the lip of the window. It was life breath, not humid or rainy. Clouds traveled this way, talking among themselves of the overcast sky to come.

So pleasant. So much a contrast to the city it breathes on. And not enough to calm my underlying jittery feeling of wanting to have it all over and done with.

Helen spoke. "We are going to a government building to talk to an official who will prepare you for the court."

At the word, "court," my tummy turned.

"She will talk to you on the questions the judge will ask. And she will give you answers that will be good for you." Helen stopped, still staring out the front windshield.

Jonathan and I exchanged a sideways glance.

Helen turned to us in the back seat. "Do you understand it?"

We nodded.

"Answers that will be good for us." Yes, I understand. They are trying to help us say the right things, to make the adoption go through. Thank you, God, that they're for us – not against us.

It was just as Helen said. The government building rose tall and plain. Inside, we met Tatiana. Tatiana spoke no English, so Helen squinted her eyes with concentration, listening attentively to Tatiana's rapid run-on sentences before turning to us to translate.

"Tonight, after our visa photo with the girl, you must go back to Igor and Valentina's apartment and create a 15-minute speech," Helen said. "Give the judge information about your life, your family, and all of the securities you have in America. You must say that it is 'in the child's best interest' to adopt this baby into your family. Do you understand?"

"Yes," we answered in unison.

"And one more thing." Helen paused and leaned forward.

"You must not forget to ask the judge to waive the ten-day wait."

Jonathan and I nodded. I breathed in a deep breath, cementing the mental check list into my head.

Though I love to write, this "speech" may be the hardest thing I've ever written.

Then the two Russian women spoke together further, popping words back and forth like popcorn. Both nodded in emphasis, briskly agreeing to whatever they spoke. The way they conversed reminded me of two chefs stirring a pot, tossing in seasonings, carefully making sure all of the ingredients were measured to a tee.

Then Helen and Tatiana turned to me.

"And don't cry. If you cry, we might cry."

Helen smiled a real smile. Tatiana nodded and closed her eyelids in one knowing nod, reflecting emotional warmth across her face. In that moment, as women, our hearts touched in understanding.

Helen quickly rose, we followed her lead, Tatiana ushered us out, and we returned to the waiting car. My emotions tried desperately to keep up with the pace.

Back at the orphanage, we greeted Allie again. This time, her recognition of us shone unmistakable. Standing in a little side room we'd never been in before, I enjoyed every second of changing Allie into a pale-pink cotton two-piece outfit for the visa photo. Jonathan sat on a wooden bench near her head, talking baby talk all the while to her as I tried to capture her wiggly feet into a pretty pair of pink socks.

I pulled the baby shoes out of my bag and held them up to Allie's feet. They rose a full inch and a half above the tips of her toes.

"I don't think she'll be wearing those for a while!" Jonathan chuckled.

I tucked the shoes back into the bag and lifted Alexandria up snug to my chest.

No shoes today, little one! We'll just have to show off those pretty pink socks! Oh, how I absolutely love having a girl!

Walking down the orphanage hallway to the door with Allie tight in my arms felt so delicious. When the door opened and fresh air blew into Allie's face, she gasped an awful, raspy sound – as if someone were jamming the air down her throat. When the mellow sunshine touched Allie's face, she flinched, fluttering her eyes in pain. Jonathan quickly pulled the corner of the blanket over Allie's face. A warm gust blew the blanket off, and a fierce squint grabbed Allie's eyes in an almost-angry scowl. We rushed to tuck the blanket over and in.

My dear Lord, she doesn't know what it's like to be outside.

Inside Victor's car, it felt completely odd not to have a car seat to protect our little baby. It felt even more odd when we realized that there were no working seatbelts in the car. I cradled Alexandria deep into my arms, mommy-protection emotions rising rapidly, ping-ponging all through my body. With each bump and jostle, my arms wrapped more tightly around her frame. Allie looked up, face outlined in innocence.

We hadn't traveled but minutes when the car stopped at the curb in front of a small storefront studio. Knowing my hands were more interested in cradling the baby, Victor ran around the car and opened the door for me. While Jonathan tucked the blanket over Allie's face,

Victor reached out and took my elbow. All of the attention rushed to this little one, this priceless treasure.

Inside the studio, an old-fashioned accordion camera perched on a tripod like a big black crow. An older gentleman waved and muttered in Russian. Helen translated.

"You sit here. You hold the baby this way." We obliged. Allie's quiet stare soaked in the surroundings.

The photographer pulled a towel over his head and the camera flashed twice before he reappeared. He made one quick nod and smiled the terse Russian smile. And then we were back in the car.

I wanted the outing to last the whole day, but sitting back in the car meant that we had to return Alexandria. In a few uncomfortable, bumpy minutes, we drove up to the orphanage.

"Do you want to walk the girl in," asked Helen, "or do you want to give her to the caregiver at the door?"

"Oh!" I said. "Please – may we go in?"

Helen nodded and we trooped up the steps, through the thick door, and down the hallway. I wanted to hold on to every second with my little one.

Once inside the room, I lay Allie on the table to change her back into the orphanage clothes. Allie lay on her back, kicking and smiling. Slowly pulling her arms from the pretty pink top, I put on a clean diaper and then slid her thin legs into the dirty-white garment. A caregiver entered the room to watch. Leaning ever-so-slightly against the wall, the caregiver held her arms straight down, one hand clasped over the front of the other at the base of her white frock. Even though I only glanced once, I knew she watched me the entire time. The caregiver's look felt curious and without feeling.

Jonathan held the carry bag open for me, and with one hand still on Allie's chest, I folded the pretty pink outfit and placed it in. Allie wasn't going anywhere; I knew she didn't roll well. I wanted to keep the lifeline of touch between us.

I reached into the bag and pulled out a few more clean diapers and handed them to the caregiver with a smile. Without a smile, she took them and nodded. Then Jonathan and I turned full attention to our little Alexandria.

With both of my hands around her body, I leaned forward to place my cheek against hers. Allie wiggled her arms and kicked her legs in excitement. I whispered in her ear, "Paka, my sweet. See you later."

Without taking my face away, I rose, lifting her body against me one last time for the day. Pulling Allie away from me, I passed her to the caregiver, handing my baby into the arms of the stranger. I blew a kiss, and we turned and walked through the doorway and down the hall.

It was time to write our speech.

Chapter Twenty-Seven

The Proceedings Begin

Pouring water from the pink glass pitcher, I filled two glasses and placed them on the wooden end table. Flopping across the futon, I rolled onto my tummy, feet dangling over the side. Jonathan sat comfortably in the stuffed chair in the corner of the bedroom.

"Don't forget to mention your grandparents living in Russia."

Not looking up, Jonathan nodded, made an "umph" sound, and scribbled.

Knuckles rapped on the bedroom door. Rising, I opened it, and there stood Valentina with a bright-red lipstick smile. She waved us toward the kitchen in her familiar wave, round arm movements echoing her round shape.

Jonathan, his hand still poised with pen over our "speech," looked up.

"I suppose we have to eat."

We were "in the groove" of writing; I hated to stop our progress. But he was right. The long day was almost over. We needed to eat dinner. And we shouldn't keep our gracious hostess waiting.

At the table, liver and noodles rose in heaping mounds on perfectly-set plates. I never liked liver. As a young girl, I tried to hide the brown stuff, bite by bite, in my napkin. I didn't dare attempt to hide it now. So I turned to Valentina smiling by the stove, patted my belly, and said, "You are feeding us so well! I am still full from earlier. Please…,"

I pinched my thumb and pointer finger down to an inch. "May I have only a small bit of food?"

Valentina understood. I guess I was getting better at my "Russian charades." She smiled, grabbed a pot, and meandered to the table to re-portion my food. Then, placing a carton of thick, creamy apricot juice on the table between our plates, Valentina moved off to the side to stand in her usual place.

The liver wasn't as bad as I remembered. Maybe it was the way Valentina prepared it. Or maybe it was because I didn't want to insult this wonderfully kind woman. Whatever the reason, I ate everything on my plate.

After dinner, we returned to our room. Jonathan and I made sure each and every one of Helen and Tatiana's points hit the page. Working together, the abrupt thoughts we threw onto paper became smooth sentences.

Then it was finished.

Jonathan stood up in the center of the room.

"Shall I try it?"

Holding the paper in the air, he looked like one of the signers of the Declaration of Independence in that famous painting on the wall of the National Archives.

"Sure. Go ahead."

I listened to Jonathan's voice rise and fall, trying to imagine standing in court. As he read, the seriousness of it all hit me.

Oh my gosh. Court is tomorrow.

A strong desire – a desire to be understood by these people, to let them know how much I absolutely loved this little girl and couldn't live a day without her – drenched my entire body.

They must understand. They absolutely MUST.

I could tell that Jonathan felt it too; his words sounded good, but as he spoke in this little bedroom, it all came out much too fast.

"Slow down, hon. Remember – Helen will be translating the whole time you're speaking."

He started again. Rollercoasters zoomed through my stomach.

I'm glad it's Jonathan, not me, who's going to be up front.

Jonathan finished and looked up, eyebrows lifted.

"I think it's good," I said.

He cocked his head.

"Really, Elle; do you think it's good?"

I nodded.

"And you'll be great."

Oh Lord, please make it so.

That night, sleep didn't come easily for either one of us. I breathed Romans 15:13 in and out of my tired body: "Now may the God of hope fill you with all joy and peace in believing, that you may abound in hope by the power of the Holy Spirit."

And the "answer" of Isaiah 25, verses 9 and 10, washed quietness over my mind: *"Those who hope in Me will not be disappointed."*

Daybreak peeled back the sky. Our third day in Arkhangelsk. The day to stand in court to formally ask the judge to allow us to become parents of a little girl. *Our little girl. Our Alexandria.*

Jonathan rolled over and kissed my cheek. Then the morning moved quickly.

In silence, we dressed into our best. While I stood in front of the bath mirror adjusting my collar, Jonathan moved in and appeared behind me. His arms slid around me in silence. We stood.

"I want it to be all done."

"Me too."

I wonder what Allie is doing.

I couldn't eat much at breakfast. Scraping our chairs back from the table, we thanked Valentina. Her compassionate glances showed me she understood.

Her husband held the same understanding. Leaving the apartment, Igor's purposeful words flowed to me in simple reassurance: "It will be oh-kayee."

'Oh-kayee.' Dear God, I so want it to be OK.

This is our moment. Please, Lord. Guide our lips. Give us the words. Calm me. Cover over me with Your comfort.

You can imagine the bubbling in my stomach when we found out that Helen and the court officials had mis-communicated.

"I am sorry," Helen apologized. "Our hearing is moved to the afternoon time. We must go back to the apartment and come back later."

Climbing into Victor's little car, taut silence made the engine sound louder and the exhaust smell extra-foul. *We were told by the agency that we would need to be flexible. I guess now's the time.*

Back at the apartment, we ate lunch in more silence. Valentina and Igor moved quietly in the shadows. Time felt like the "early days" back home, waiting and waiting, biding time to get to the end moment.

We finished and excused ourselves to our room.

Jonathan spent the time reading our speech, whispering the words to himself, closing his eyes in thought. My nerves dangled as a frayed piece of yarn blowing in irritated jerks in the wind.

I tried to stretch out on the bed to relax. It wasn't working. I tried to relax the muscles in my arms and legs one by one, in Lamaze pacing. It still wasn't working.

"Jonathan?"

"Yes?"

My voice scraped high and thin. "What if the judge says we can't adopt her?"

Once spoken, the weight of my question pushed thousands of pounds into the air we breathed.

Jonathan moved over to the bed and to my side. He laid his body out next to mine, and he wrapped his arms around me. We snuggled in silence.

A strong, rhythmic "bap-bap-bap-bap" hit the door, and my body jumped. We must have dozed off. Jonathan's arm, heavy and warm, rose off mine. Fuzzy, we slid to sit on the edge of the bed together.

"Hallo…" Helen spoke through the door. "It is time to go again."

We smoothed our crinkled clothes and gathered our things.

Back in the car, I tried to push the thickness from my mind and body. The sights and sounds around us, bumping along in the car, felt somehow familiar but incredibly eccentric, almost outlandish. It all pulled me forward in surreal strides.

And then we were there.

The courtroom's dim light felt hollow. Its cool wood and stone loomed intimidating before me. The tall wooden door closed behind us in a dull thud, and we walked down the dark hallway. The stale, closed-up-room smell and dim light gave the distinct feeling of walking into a tomb.

As we followed Helen, only our heels made conversation on the dark linoleum. My eyes adjusted and details emerged, giving clearer edges to the straight lines of the plain windows, walls, and doorways. Deeper into the cavernous building, the floor looked more worn and scratched with each step. Though it was warm and sunny outside, every one of the window panes stared at us, tightly shut.

We passed a woman dressed in a stiff, formal black pencil dress and some men with baggy black pants and rumpled white shirts rumbling serious Russian.

Then we entered the court room. I didn't think it possible, but when the door closed behind us, we stood in even thicker silence. We filed across and sat in hard wooden chairs in the front row, only six feet from the judge's bench. Already in the room, the orphanage director sat nearby. Tatiana sat in the back of the room. Next to Tatiana sat the woman who had fixed the typewriter in the orphanage. *Strange, that she is here.*

A woman in a suit entered, bellowing what must have been our American equivalent to, "All rise." We stood with a chorus of chairs-scraping and clothes-rustling. In walked a female judge draped in black.

The judge sat behind the tall wooden desk with an aloof disinterest. Behind her, on the wall, loomed an official Russian symbol of some kind or another. Helen moved to stand between us and the judge's desk, so close that, if I wanted to, I could have reached out and touched Helen's black polyester skirt.

Then the judge spoke. Her disinterest turned to intensity. Thick Russian words rolled and spat and mumbled back and forth, hitting the hard walls and floors like cold, rhythmic waves on Lake Ontario. We continued to sit as words moved back and forth with Helen. The seat felt hard. I shuffled my feet.

Helen spoke in systematic confidence. Then the orphanage director stood where she was and spoke, informing the official in English that she "comes on behalf of the child" – measuring her words in that same kind of orderly self-reliance. Then the director spoke in Russian.

We followed the soliloquy with Helen's help; Helen sat next to us, whispering abrupt interpretations in our ears, abbreviations of the rising and falling dialogue punctuated in and around us.

Then the Typewriter Fixer Woman came forward. She stood directly in front of us, her back tall and stiff. According to Helen, she spoke on our behalf – stating that we had bonded with the child and took good care of her.

Oh my gosh! I feel like I've been in a James Bond movie! This woman spied on us while we innocently bonded with our baby!

Then the judge turned and faced me. Her words punctuated the air like darts whizzing past my ears.

Helen looked directly into my eyes, and a feeling of dread rose in my stomach.

Helen whispered, "She wants you to come forward."

Chapter Twenty-Eight

Courtroom Intensity

My mouth went dry. I stood to my feet and looked at Helen standing beside, so close I could almost feel the fibers of her woolen jacket. Helen nodded.

My body started trembling.

Helen spoke to the judge in Russian. Her melodic sentence rose and fell in a clear, distinct pulse. She nodded back toward me and, with open hand nearly brushing my ear, concluded, "Elle Conner."

"Canner?" asked the judge.

"Conner," corrected Helen.

"Conner or Canner?" asked the judge again.

"Cooooooner," answered Helen again, stretching out the "o" as if talking to a toddler.

Satisfied, the judge turned straight to me, shoulders squared. From the judge's mouth flew a string of measured words, connected together with shards of irritation.

Helen turned with a funny look on her face and translated.

"The questions is, 'Why do you want this child when you already have two children?'"

Horror filled the pit of my stomach and ran up my spine, thrusting a crushing jab of panic into my heart.

Oh God, help me! She doesn't understand.

Am I going to lose my baby?

My legs shook. Tears gushed. I knew I had to speak, but invisible hands squeezed and choked my throat.

Gathering all the energy I could, I forced air past my vocal chords.

"Your honor," came quiet words from a voice.

Was that my voice?

"I have met the girl, love her, and want to take her home."

Then I fell apart.

Sobbing uncontrollably, my body took over. I wanted to stop crying but couldn't. The emotions of months of longing, working, and waiting spilled – surging, rushing, in siege over my whole being.

The judge excused me to sit.

Somewhere far away, I felt Jonathan's hand holding mine.

I must stop. I must stop. I must stop crying.

There. On the side of the wall, over there. There's a window.

What's outside?

I forced myself to look through the glass.

A large tree. Is it a maple? Or is it an oak? The tree is firm. The tree is solid. I can be like the tree. The tree has roots. My roots are in the Lord my God.

God, give me strength.

As I focused outside the window, the inside of the room became clear. My tears slowed. The judge had called Jonathan forward. And now, in strength, Jonathan performed our speech brilliantly.

Next, the judge shot questions at Jonathan. Helen translated and Jonathan answered. The volley continued for I-don't-know-how-many slow-motion minutes. My tears stopped pouring down my face, and the trembling dissipated into my wooden seat, filling my limbs with wobbly Jello®. In order to mask the wavering, I fidgeted.

And I needed to go to the bathroom.

"Why don't you want to adopt from your country?"

"What are your plans for your future?"

"What will happen if the husband can no longer work?"

The relentless, rapid-fire questions didn't cease. And with each query-bullet, an unusual sensation surfaced and formed a shape my mind. It was the emerging shape of the truth.

God, I see it. I hear it. Beneath the judge-woman's granite-hard exterior, she really cares.

Then the volley changed.

The judge spoke again, and Helen echoed, "No one came to visit the baby during the months she was in the orphanage. That entitles her to be classified as an 'orphan,' making her eligible for adoption."

Those words ripped the edge of my heart.

The judge continued, and Helen echoed translation.

"You will need to sign a document. You must check off number one, the birth parents are deceased, or number two, the birth parents have abandoned the child. You must decide. But we recommend you check the box labeled 'deceased.'"

They want me to lie. I can't do that. It's not in the core of who I am.

The "instructions" finished, and the judge excused herself and left the room.

The hearing had lasted almost an hour. And then there we all sat, quietly waiting. "Nervous" is too weak of a word to describe it.

Unnerved. Intimidated. Anxious. Alarmed. Scared. Fearful. Distressed.

All those words combined together look black and white, compared to the color of that moment.

Then Helen motioned for Tatiana and the Typewriter Fixer Woman to join us in the front of the bench in the middle of the room.

We began to talk. Quietly at first. Then in normal tones. I found myself giggling a silly sort of giggle at Tatiana's mimicking of the judge: "Well is it Caaaanner or Coooonner?"

The side door opened; the woman in the suit came in and spoke another half-shout to the edges of the room.

"The judge is coming," Helen translated.

Intensity filled the room, sending us scurrying to original places. The judge entered and strode to sit with bravado atop her perch behind the desk.

"This adoption hearing," translated Helen from the judge, "will be kept a secret in the country of Russia. It is complete."

Helen paused to allow the judge to speak.

Straight faced, Helen echoed, "Congratulations. Good luck. And goodbye."

The judge promptly picked up a file of papers and, without a glance, strode out of the room.

That's it? Oh – Oh, my!

The atmosphere exploded into relief beyond relief; Jonathan and I threw our arms around each other. Joy burst in new tears from our eyes.

I've never cried so much in my entire life, as much as I've cried over the last nine months!

"It was not good to have crying!" Tatiana scolded, brow deep. "But I like you. It is okay."

"Yes," said Helen, all smiles. "It is very good! You have given a good job, especially with this tough judge."

Squeezing hands, Jonathan and I beamed.

"We call her The Vampire," laughed Helen. "She is not a happy woman, and we think it is because her husband must not satisfy her!"

Everyone burst out laughing. As Helen covered her mouth in mock surprise, Jonathan let out a deep belly laugh.

With light steps, we gathered our things and scampered down the hallway and out the door. To our surprise, outside on the steps of the courthouse stood Kirill.

What's Kirill doing here?! How did he get here from St. Petersburg? Oh my! Like Dorothy in "The Wizard of Oz" – People come and go quickly around here!

Kirill wasn't interested in greetings and pleasantries. He wanted the low-down.

"How did it go?" he asked, looking into Helen's face.

"She cried!" Helen answered with a smile.

Kirill winked in my direction. Then, throwing his arms around me, then Jonathan, he bellowed, "Congratulations!"

We all turned and walked a short way to Victor, still waiting patiently at the car parked at the curb.

Kirill and Helen chattered; Victor and the other women chattered.

Jonathan and I didn't say a word.

My words, my emotions, and my energy – they were simply all used up. I felt too jostled and jumbled to understand my own feelings. And words, sentences…even the thought process that goes into speaking….

In a time like this, they were utterly useless. Totally unnecessary. Absolutely impotent.

"Come," said Helen, motioning toward the car door Victor held open.

"It is finished. It is time to go and get your daughter. For good."

We climbed into the car and Victor merged into the traffic. And all I could hear were reverberations of Helen's last words: *It is finished...For good.*

No more waiting. No more hoops to jump through. No more questions and wonderings and worries. Alexandria Rose, you are ours.

Thank you, God! Thank you, thank you, God!

Chapter Twenty-Nine

The Baby Room

Walking into the orphanage this time, we didn't go to the little room down the hall. We followed Helen straight to The Baby Room – the room where Alexandria Rose spent the entirety of her little life.

"Proceed in to find your daughter," said Helen, her hand guiding us gently past the paint-chipped door frame.

I wasn't ready for the room's harsh and horrible reality.

From every corner of the room, dozens of vacant, hollow eyes turned in unison. The sunny white glow emanating from the tall, tightly-shut lace-curtained windows caused tufts of baby hair, rumpled clothing, and stick-like limbs to stand out in phantom silhouette. The atmosphere felt soaked with the stench of dirty clothes, urine, porridge, and weak disinfectant.

In the center of the plain tile floor laid a rug. On the rug lay babies. Ten of them. Scattered about. With sunken eyes and unanswered whimpers.

The sound pierced my soul. My body began to ache.

A caregiver methodically shuffled from one child to the next. Some babies had rolled off the rug and onto the hard linoleum floor. With no movement in their bodies, they lay there and cried pitifully.

My eyes flew across the room.

Most of the children made no sound at all.

Every single one blinked at me with globed eyes, dull and empty of innocence.

To the side, a caregiver fed an infant propped in a chair at a wooden table. I couldn't look away. Something wasn't right.

Oh! The caregiver is standing behind the baby, facing the child's back!

Both baby and caregiver looked blankly in the same direction at some nebulous horizon point.

The caregiver reached from behind the baby to the bowl on the table. Scooping broth from the bowl with one of those big tablespoons, she moved the watery brew in bored, mechanical movement into the baby's mouth.

The caregiver looks as if manipulating parts on an assembly line. The baby opened and closed its mouth in resolute, emotionless gulps.

Then, from the table, the baby looked up. Her little eyes peered into me in emptiness.

My breaths came deeper and heavier. My chest felt pressed.

To the opposite side, another caregiver woman stood at a work basin washing baby clothes. She held a worn sleeper between white knuckles. Back and forth she squished and pressed the sleeper into the water in the basin, her mouth and brow pressed in flat, parallel lines. The woman's attention flicked at us for only a second, her face showing no emotion. She concentrated on the mound of soiled clothing towering next to the basin.

I saw no diapers on the pile. And glancing around the room again, there were no poofy bottoms on the babies to give away the presence of such a luxury as a diaper – only saggy clothing hanging on tiny limbs. Some babies wore extra pants and sleepers.

I watched the woman on the rug. Folding a shirt into a rectangle, she promptly pinned the bundle around and between skinny little legs stuck up into the air – a hopeful creation to keep urine from running onto the floor.

From the smell of things, it didn't work too well.

Facing the side wall, I gasped. There, five little babies – stripped of clothing, completely naked – sat balancing on buckets. All ten of their little hands lay folded under their chins as if praying.

Motionless. Emotionless. Waiting. Trying to fulfill the caregivers' hopes that they'd go potty rather than soil their clothes.

Miracle in the City of Angels

Unbelievable! These babies are less than a year old! Look at their little feet dangling off the edge of those buckets – My God, they look terrified!

My Dear Lord, where are these babies' parents? Were the parents just children themselves? Or were these children just tossed away because of "inconvenience"?

So many babies! Twenty-four, maybe? All under the age of one. And three women to care for them. And Helen. And Jonathan. And me. And the sensation of an ugly apparition permeating the air.

A tremor ran through my core. Nausea squished and pressed in my stomach, jerking in tandem with the rhythm of the clothes shoved back and forth in the wash basin.

From one corner of the room to the next corner, my eyes desperately searched for any kind of affection – for love, for tenderness, for a laugh, a tickle, or a smile. Anything!

Blank stares looked back.

Dreadfulness trickled into my arteries like cold IV fluid. When the feeling hit my heart, a passionate yearning to do something – anything – for these other little ones swelled.

How do I just stand here and not pick up a child in need? I want to carry them all home. How can we have such a pleasant life – and know that these babies are here?

Jonathan turned to me. "How many babies are we taking home?"

Dear God, Jonathan feels it too.

And then I saw her. There, across the room, a caregiver carried a baby facing outward. They were moving toward the wash basin.

Ah! Our daughter!

But instead of a wonderful rush of joy for this moment – this oh-so-long-awaited-moment – Jonathan's words began an avalanche of heaviness caving into my soul. I wanted to reach, to touch, to comfort each one of these children.

But I can't, Lord! I'm only one!

Look at all these children! Oh God! Look at these desperate babies! How can we take just one and walk away from all these other little ones? Standing here, deep in the presence of these tiny, precious babies who wait, all alone – the horror of it rises –

Oh my God, look at them!

The hollow eyes continued to stare, blinking. A girl-baby coughed a wet cough. Her body convulsed once, then lay still to stare into space with watery eyes. On the rug, pitiful, haunting baby-cries wailed from one child, then another.

My emotions rushed into feelings of hopelessness.

How will I walk away from this, knowing I'll never return? How will I take just Allie and leave all of these beautiful ones behind? How? How am I going to do this?

My Lord, who will love these babies? Who will hold them tonight? And tomorrow? And the next night? Who will wipe away their tears? Who will rock them to sleep? Oh Lord, My God – What if no one comes? What if no one takes them home? What will happen to these precious lives?

If no one comes, what will happen as their cries become a dull ache that no one soothes? And with years upon years of living here.... What will happen as they're turned to the streets to fend for themselves?

Look at this beautiful little girl! Has anyone touched her cheek with love? Has anyone kissed this little boy's forehead and tickled his cheek with eyelashes? That baby's arms are trembling with his cries! Isn't anyone there who will take him into their arms to calm and soothe his shaking body?

I was deliriously happy to come here and hold my precious baby. But now, as I'm about to take my baby from this place, all of these little eyes pierce deeply into my heart – and it rips my insides apart.

Oh, Dear Lord! Every day, every hour, every second – Oh, how your heart must hurt! Oh, how you must long to have your families open their hearts and embrace these little ones!

Please send a mommy! A mommy who will give her heart in unabashed love! Send a daddy! A daddy who will courageously stand strong and brave as a father!

My heart wept as it had never wept before.

Will anyone come for them?

Chapter Thirty

Baptism with our Russian Five

"Come," said Helen.

Somehow, I closed my mind to the other babies. I had to strictly focus on Allie and our future with her.

Jonathan and I walked to stand at the side of the basin. Removing Allie's clothing, the caregiver lay her clothes, all stitched with "#4" at the collar, on the side table. Picking up Allie under the arms, she held Allie inside the basin, tossing water across her half-limp body. In the cool wetness, Allie's hanging limbs stiffened. The caregiver lifted Allie, dripping, and wrapped a towel around her torso; then she laid her naked body on the table and stepped back.

"Go ahead," said Helen. "Dress your daughter."

Presented with my naked baby, it felt like I'd just given birth.

I leaned over and kissed Alexandria's tummy, then her forehead, then her nose. The dullness left Allie's eyes, and she wriggled and kicked.

Reaching in the carry bag with my free hand, I pulled out a bright white undershirt and placed it over Allie's head. With her face covered for a second, Allie's breaths gasped. Her head popped gently out of the shirt, and then she smiled and gasped some more.

Out of the bag came a package-fresh pink sleeper with the word, "Sweetheart," embroidered on the smock. Allie's arms and legs kicked and pumped – so different from the dullness that shrouded her body in the basin, just minutes before. Next to me, Jonathan played the role of proud papa, catching on video Alexandria Rose's "birth" into our family.

"We made it!" I breathed into Allie's neck. "You are my daughter now, and we're going to take you home. There are so many people waiting to meet you, precious one."

Allie gurgled and smiled. Tying the bonnet under her chin, I realized she knew us, now. And she looked picture-perfect in her brand new clothes.

"Helen," I asked. "Before we leave, may we photograph Alexandria with her caregiver and the orphanage doctor?"

Helen translated our request to the caregiver standing nearby. The caregiver's eyebrows rose in pleasant-but-suspicious surprise; but she nodded in agreement, straightening her white smock with broad hands to get ready for the impromptu portrait.

"Tell her we believe the pictures will be a special addition in Allie's baby book, to help represent the first year of her life."

Helen translated again. The caregiver lifted her brow – again. Apparently, pictures and baby books documenting these kinds of things were new concepts.

So we stood next to the caregiver with Allie and snapped a smiling photo, and then another, while Allie stared in interest and the caregiver smiled without showing her teeth. Then, on a quick word from Helen, the orphanage doctor came into the room, and we snapped some more pictures like the first.

It felt just like the photos we'd taken in the delivery room with Thomas and Michael. The nurses and doctors whom we barely knew played a somewhat-significant role in bringing our child to us, and so we snapped pictures. The caregivers and orphanage personnel played an important role, too. It was the role of holding the door open, for us to step through together as a new family.

For a split second, I thought of asking for a piece of Allie's #4 clothing. Maybe they'd give us the booties she wore that day. But then I looked around the room. The babies still lay in the same spots. I heard their cries and saw their eyes. And the thought flickered away.

These babies desperately need to keep every stitch of clothing here. And more.

We walked away from that room, holding our beautifully-dressed baby in our arms.

I looked back. And in that moment of looking back, the strongest feeling I've ever felt coursed through me. It was a rush – a rich and horrible feeling. A fervent passion, like fiery zeal, scorching into my soul. The sight, smell, and sounds seared into me. I could taste the pain in that room. The bittersweet of that incredible moment became palpable, so clear and vivid.

I'll never forget.

We drove away. Baby in arms. Bumping along the road in the little car. Gazing now into my Alexandria's face. Her eyes wide. In awe? No, fear.

Dear Lord, the look on her face is one of shock. This is only the second time my baby has been in a car. So strange; she doesn't know the feeling of being in a car...something we so take for granted as "normal." I wonder how many "normal" pieces of my life will be strange – and fearful – for my new daughter.

When we arrived at the apartment, Igor and Valentina greeted us with smiles and outreached arms. They cooed and made "ttchu, ttchu" sounds of Russian baby talk, with lovely Russian phrases running back and forth. Kirill, Helen, and Victor stood in the small apartment like proud family, nodding and raising eyebrows while obviously recounting the courtroom tension. Here they stood, our "Russian Five" – Helen, Valentina, Igor, Victor, and Kirill.

"Helen, Victor, and Kirill." Jonathan's roll call quieted the room. "It is important to us that we baptize our new daughter right away. Our pastor has counseled me on performing the baptismal right of our faith. Will you stay to witness the event?"

God entrusted Alexandria into our care. We entrusted her back to Him. And these five people helped make it happen. It only made sense to include them all.

But will our new friends be offended, thinking we're "pushing" our faith on them?

"Yes, please," I added. "Igor and Valentina – may we use your living room? Is it alright?"

Helen translated to Victor and Valentina. All heads solemnly bobbed in agreement. I knew they didn't understand the meaning of what was about to take place. But from the looks on our faces and the tone of our voices, they understood that something very important was about to happen.

Helen, Igor, Valentina, and Victor sat lined up on the couch, side by side. Sinking into the old springs, hands folded properly, they looked more like four teenagers waiting for the first dance. Kirill sat down in the single chair, comfortably crossing one knee over the other. Kirill's mellow acceptance made me feel more at ease.

Jonathan and I stood. I held Allie.

All eyes fixed on Alexandria Rose.

I placed tiny Allie in Jonathan's broad arms. His hands trembled. Stepping to my suitcase, I pulled from the side pocket a photocopied page from our Lutheran hymnal back home. Holding the page up for Jonathan to read, my hands shook too, and the page quivered.

"Dear Lord, we stand here today to baptize our beautiful new daughter in Your Name..."

The sound of Jonathan's voice fell into the totally-quiet room, and the small space became vibrant with the presence of God. Our Russian Five blinked in awe as Jonathan spoke and Helen translated. The words pressed quietly through the air, like footsteps on soft grass, rising and falling in step with my breaths and Allie's small movements.

Jonathan dipped his fingers into the Russian water and made the sign of the cross on Allie's forehead and then over her heart.

"In the name of the Father." Allie blinked and looked into Jonathan's eyes. He moved his fingers into the water and again over her forehead and heart.

"And of the Son." Jonathan's voice cracked. I blinked away tears. Jonathan made the sign again, one more time, on her forehead and over her heart.

"And of the Holy Spirit. Amen." Jonathan swallowed hard and closed his eyes, cradling Allie. At my prompting, each of our Russian friends stood and silently, one by one, signed the "witness" lines on the baptismal certificate.

The murmur of Russian conversation returned, and we moved to the kitchen. Valentina began pulling pots and spoons to the counter to prepare dinner.

Jonathan and I slipped aside.

I held Allie close. Jonathan wrapped his arm under mine, and the two of us stood, touching. Our breath moved in and out together. Neither said a word. Allie's eyelids fell closed.

This is our child. Our exquisite gift from God.

Chapter Thirty-One

Goodbye to the City of Angels

Our first night with our daughter was less than perfect. Valentina fixed a nest of blankets on the floor next to our bed for Allie. But when placed in the nest, Allie wiggled and fussed. Everything – sights, smells, touches, tastes – was terribly different. And her little body and mind rebelled.

I picked Allie up to rock her, but she arched her back and squirmed. Valentina swooped in and scooped Allie from my arms. Patting Allie's bottom as if scolding her for misbehaving in front of her new parents, Valentina chattered, "Spot, spot, spot, spot," meaning, "Sleep, sleep."

It took a long time to pat away the turmoil in our little one. Eventually, she fell asleep and Valentina tucked her under the folds.

I felt strangely impotent as a mother.

Though it was past summer solstice, the White Nights still filled the sky, causing me to lunge in and out of sleep. During these special weeks of the year, the sun doesn't descend below the horizon enough for the sky to grow dark in St. Petersburg. The city's latitude is too high for the night to fall. So during the White Nights, the city seems as in daylight, no matter what the time of day. Tonight, the sun didn't set until after ten; the eerie atmosphere dawdled, with no intention of leaving. In that place between awake and asleep, my mind half-dreamed visions of the city, the orphanage, and the faces of children. Rest never fully came.

I awoke to Allie's fussing noises.

"Jonathan?" I whispered.

No answer.

The sky brightening, I picked up Allie and walked to the kitchen.

How odd. Usually by this time in the morning, Valentina has breakfast ready.

"Well, little Alexandria," I said. "I know how to cook. Let's get going."

I peered around the kitchen.

"You must be hungry. Let's take care of you first. Now where does Valentina keep that hot cereal stuff..."

Still dressed in her rumpled nighty, Valentina's sudden entrance interrupted our mother-daughter conversation.

"Schu..." she muttered under her breath, followed by a string of mottled, sputtering Russian. With arms pushing broadly in brushing movements – a bit like I was a huge dust bunny to be brushed out the door – she tried shooing me out of the kitchen.

Why is she pushing me out like this? Why can't I be the one to fix a meal for Allie?

With a tsk-tsking finger, Valentina pointed out the window. Then she nodded toward the clock.

3 AM! Oh my gosh –The White Nights...

My neck turned three shades of red. I smiled a weak smile and took Allie back to the bedroom.

When Helen showed up five hours later and I explained what happened, we all laughed about it together. Originally, I felt quite foolish. But I had to let it all go. Strange customs, strange land. As Cindy said, "Expect everything different. And don't get bent out of shape about anything."

Jonathan returned to the bedroom to begin packing.

I walked to the kitchen and Valentina brought us a bowl of the oatmeal-like hot cereal. With no baby seat or high chair, I held Allie on my lap. Valentina scooped the gruel into her mouth.

The strange feeling returned.

After Allie finished eating, Igor picked her up and took her away from us, to the living room. Placing her on a blanket on the floor, he clicked on the 50's-style TV and sat down to stare at the newsman. On

Miracle in the City of Angels

the floor, Allie fussed. Jonathan joined me in the kitchen, and together we sat to eat. But the food stuck in my throat.

My ears heard my daughter's voice. My eyes saw my child's fitful movements. And my legs itched to move.

I pushed back my chair and walked to Allie.

"Tsk! Tsk!" scolded Igor with a half-smile. "You Americans hold babies too much."

I didn't care what he thought. Allie experienced too many days without a mother's touch. I picked her up.

Allie looked into my eyes and settled.

I am your mother. It's time for me to do what I know is right.

And from there on out, that's the attitude I held. I knew our Russian friends were trying to be helpful. Their kindness spilled out everywhere we turned. But at this point, their good intentions needed to be ignored. Now it was my time to be Momma.

While finishing packing, I was in charge of Allie. And while presenting gifts to our friends, I was in charge of Allie.

We gave candies, cookies, and nuts. We unfolded Detroit Red Wings t-shirts and hats, along with a photo of Igor Larionov carrying the Stanley Cup through Red Square. And I presented a gift bag full of Michigan post cards, soaps, lotions, shampoo, and candles.

Jonathan handed Igor an ice scraper.

"What is this?" he said. We chuckled and explained, and he ran his hands over the edge with a grin. Thinking it a toy, Allie reached from my arms to the scraper, and we laughed again.

This is the right time to give them the package from Molly and Rob.

Igor and Valentina beamed at the pictures of Katie. And, remembering that first day in Molly, Rob, and Katie's home, longing to hold my little one, I held onto my Allie tighter.

Presents strewn around the couch and floor, our friends fingered and turned and smelled the gifts.

"Igor, may we use your telephone to call home?"

"Michael," I said, excited to hear his little voice. "How are you? Oh, I miss you and love you!"

"Mommy, Grandma took us to McDonalds', and I got a toy!"

I smiled. Michael was just fine.

"Hey – here's Allie! Talk to your new sister!"

I held the phone up to Allie's ear, and Michael's voice squeaked, "Helllooooo Allie!"

Allie turned to look at the receiver with a look of confusion. Jonathan and I laughed, so Allie smiled.

"We're coming home, sweetie. We'll see you very, very soon – in just a couple of days. We have to go to Moscow now, and then we'll fly across the ocean and come home!"

Michael peeped, "OK, Mom. Do you want to talk to Grandma?"

I could hear relief in Mom's voice. A few more days. Just a few more days, and we'd be back.

And after the phone call, a gentle knock on the door told me Victor was ready to take us to the airport. Bags packed, Allie dressed in fresh clothes – there we stood in bittersweet goodbye.

I took a breath. The smell of black tea steeping on the stove filled my nostrils. Helen motioned for us to sit in the living room together, one last time.

I looked at Helen. Her high-heeled black shoes peeked from beneath black dress pants. Her printed silk shirt lay professionally against her body. Her hair lay combed neatly, just as it had been all week. She really was beautiful. More than that, my time with this woman showed her beautiful spirit and tender heart toward helping the little children safely connect with families. *What a wonderful woman.*

Sitting on the couch, Victor's gentle spirit shone through. *What kind eyes. He really enjoyed this family-making too.*

Jonathan moved our luggage to the narrow hallway by the door as I spread a pastel baby blanket on the floor. One last time I placed Allie on the blanket, on her back. The center of attention, she kicked and waved, watching her fists bob in front of her face.

Igor and Valentina served tea. We sipped, savoring the moment.

Their job was complete. Our quest in The City of Angels was finished. We all felt spiritually full, like the glow after Christmas dinner.

I pulled the Journal from the side of my carry bag. I hadn't written much while here. But I didn't mind. Really, there was no time to write…only time to experience and soak in the breath and fire of the moment. Now, holding my Journal, it was once again my friend, my confidant, and inner words overflowed in my head, running into my fingers. And I knew that once home, I would write and write and write in uncontrollable runoff of the flood of rich experience and feeling absorbing my being.

But now, I needed to ask a question.

"Dear friends." My words felt big in this small apartment.

"This is a precious book. This is my Journal of our adoption. It holds writings to Alexandria that, someday, I know she will read. I'm writing this book because I want my daughter to know all that we went through to get to her. I want her to know how much we longed for her and worked for her to come home to us. I want her to know the feelings and thoughts that we experienced. And I want her to know of her country, her city, and..." I paused. A lump formed in my throat. Jonathan nodded, moving my words forward.

"...And of you. You are important people to us. Would you please write a letter to Alexandria, right now, in this book?"

Helen translated in quiet Russian. I picked up Allie and kissed her cheek. Valentina nodded and dabbed the corner of her eye with her sleeve. Igor's mouth twitched into a shy smile. Victor looked like he swallowed a goat.

Helen spoke a few more words, the five nodded, and Helen rose. And she wrote:

July 8
You are very special because your parents are special. I happy we became friends with them. I know you will have a wonderful life, it starts today. We are so happy your future is safe now. Come and see us one day.
Helen, Grandma Valentina, Grandpa Igor, and Uncle Victor

Helen swallowed the last bit of her tea and reached into her purse and pulled out something wrapped in tissue.

"Here. Here is something for you." Helen unwrapped the tissue and gently placed a pair of crystal swans into my palm.

"They are mates for life. Like you and Jonathan. If one swan breaks, you must break the other, since they cannot live without each other."

Stepping forward, Victor reached from a bag and pulled out two crystal glasses. An elegant gift from a humble and unassuming man. With one nod, his silence spoke tomes to me.

Igor handed us a map of Arkhangelsk and some post cards. We nodded and hugged. Slipping our gifts into our carry bags, then tucking the baby blanket inside, Jonathan and I followed Helen and Victor to the door. Victor took our bags to the car, and as Helen stood, door open, we turned to face our friends.

"Valentina," I said. "You are Alexandria's Russian Babushka." She smiled, understanding without translation. Leaning forward, she planted a bright red lipstick kiss on Allie's cheek.

In the heaviness of knowing we would probably never see these dear people again, I balanced Allie on my hip to hug Valentina. She looked at me with deep, genuine concern. *How she truly cares for these babies!*

Igor, next to Valentina, barely waited for his wife to step back before he pulled me towards him. My cheek brushed his white, wavy hair as I patted his back. Pulling away, he kissed Allie on the cheek.

All week, Jonathan and Valentina hadn't been physically that near to each other. Now, when Jonathan hugged Valentina, the difference in their height made Valentina giggle, and she held her hand high above her head to indicate how much taller he was than she.

Jonathan and Igor shook hands – one of those pumping kinds of shakes – and then pulled arms together to hug, still holding the handshake, cheek to cheek, thumping each other on the back.

We stepped away, waving and saying goodbye. A tear rolled down my already damp face.

Tears of sadness, tears of joy, tears of overwhelm, tears of fear, tears of gratefulness....Lord, I didn't know this many tears existed!

"I'll write and find a way to get letters back to you, I promise." And then I spoke a phrase practiced silently all week: "Bolshoi spaseebo, moy droogee."

A big thank you, my dear friends.

Spoken, these words were not enough. But they were all I had.

From the looks on Igor and Valentina's faces, the words were just fine.

Chapter Thirty-Two

Moscow

At the airport, beliefs about adoption became clear. Some people walked past us and folded their hands in prayer. With bowed heads, speaking unfamiliar words in whispery murmurs, their look of praise wrapped in lack of understanding. Others glared at us suspiciously, as if we were going to eat the child.

Like a royal escort, Helen and Kirill ushered us through the crowd, unfazed by reactions around us. We moved to the front of the line, hoisted our bags to be checked, and stood watching the woman behind the counter hand-write our tickets. Allie stared, dazed, mouth open, holding on to me with tight fists grasping my shirt.

I shifted Allie on my hip and turned toward Helen.

Oh, I wish there were some way to allow this dear woman to remain a part of my life forever. I so wish she could watch Allie grow. I wish Allie could get to know her.

Seeing the emotions on my face, Helen's eyes softened. She placed her hand on Allie's back.

"It is this little child that gives my life purpose. To see her in such a lovely family – yes, that makes my life worth living."

With her cheek on mine, we embraced one last time. Then, with noise and movement flowing around us, Jonathan and I picked up our carry-ons and entered the flow of bodies. Turning, I caught sight of the back of Helen's coiffed hair just before we walked out the door to the bus waiting to drive us far out onto a sea of cement runway, to the plane.

From there to Moscow, everything moved slower than I would have liked. Walking up the stairs of the plane, everyone stared at us. It was obvious we were the Americans with the adopted baby. Two hours on the rickety plane with people gawking curiously – it was an emotional challenge, to say the least. After landing in Moscow and meeting our facilitator and driver, Sergei, I fell into the car emotionally and physically weary.

But something inside started brightening. I couldn't help but feel "free." We were on our own, as a family, in the momentum of going home. It was the moment when the sun starts to fall low enough in the sky to begin casting golden hues on a day well-spent.

Hotel Ukrania loomed luscious to me. Tall, dark-wood doors, thick red carpets, large entryways, large rooms....I didn't care that the room boasted only two single beds again. I didn't care that the hotel didn't offer a crib. Small potatoes! I emptied every stitch of clothing from my suitcase, lay it flat, stuffed it with a big pillow, and ta-da! A mini-bed for my little daughter.

At this point in the trip, I felt like a mountain climber viewing the peak. I knew we'd make it.

I placed exhausted Alexandria, now sleeping on my shoulder, into the "bed." We sat there on the floor, staring at her every breath. We giggled with every cute noise she made.

Allie sighed in sleep.

"You can't put a price on this," said Jonathan.

I looked into his proud daddy eyes and basked. We rested in the afternoon's lull.

It's a bit dark in here. It would be nice to let some light into our room.

Rising, I drew back the thick, rubber-backed curtain and stepped back, startled. There, instead of beautiful scenery or sunshine, rose a cement wall marked with an incredibly-large symbol of the former Soviet Union – the hammer and sickle surrounded by wheat.

I closed the shade and sat down on the bed.

How poignant.

Jonathan came over and rubbed my back. "Pretty interesting."

I smiled a weak smile.

"Yeah. And pretty intimidating."

Allie stirred.

"I'm hungry, Jonathan."

"Me too."

Allie opened her eyes.

"Let's find something to eat."

"Sounds good to me."

Allie started making noise.

We changed Allie's diaper and headed out.

It was Saturday, now later in the day, and stepping from the hotel doors, the droves of people walking here and there around us made the air swim with movement.

It didn't take long to spy the little café across the street. Since the road swarmed terribly busy with cars, we used the underground walk way to get there. In the tunnel, a man sat playing his balalaika – a Russian guitar. As we approached, he stopped playing and stared. Or should I say, glared. Apparently, we offended him as adoptive parents, and he was going to let us know about it.

Seated at the café, the waitress babbled in Russian – probably the special of the day. We didn't understand a word.

"English?" I asked.

"Nyet."

I looked at Jonathan.

"Hmm," Jonathan raised his eyebrows as he always did. "Guess we should order in Russian."

This should be interesting!

Jonathan took his best stab at reading the menu. The waitress squiggled her nose, somewhat irritated, and quirked her mouth into a smile of pity. I sounded-out my best slow-motion Russian, and she scribbled a note on her pad, nodded, and left. I'm not sure what we ordered, but it came back chicken and potatoes.

Allie loved everything. Sitting on my lap, she slurped and gulped in glee.

Leaving the café to head back to our hotel room, I glanced to the side of the exit. There, sitting on a stool on the sidewalk, an old woman peeled potatoes for the next customer.

A woman peeling potatoes for all to see. How very different.
I miss home.

Though we slept fitfully that night, I awoke with anticipation. It was Sunday. We had a full day before going to the embassy for Allie's exit visa. And Sergei promised a day of sightseeing.

I love sightseeing!

Red Square, St. Basil's Cathedral, Lenin's tomb – so fascinating and exotic! Jonathan was a trooper. I knew he enjoyed the sights too, but not as much as I did. And Allie – Oh, Allie! I'm sure she was in shock. First of all, she had difficulty breathing the fresh air. It wasn't cold, but we had to keep a blanket over her most of the time. Once in a while, Sergei said, "Stop here to make a picture," and we'd quickly uncover her little head, snap the photo, and bundle her up again. All the while, she had a look on her face of stunned bemusement.

I know it sounds crazy, but the highlight of my day was visiting Vaganovskoye Cemetery. There I stood at Sergei Grinkov's grave, the resting place of the Olympic pairs skater who died at age 28 of a heart attack.

Yes, I'm "a romantic." I suppose you know that, by now. I adored Sergei and Ekaterina Gordeeva's skill together and followed their career religiously. Sergei's death made an impression on me. An impression of caring for the ones we love, because we never know when our time on this earth will be through.

We passed graves encircled with ornate fences – of poets, authors, and athletes. Then there was Sergei's stone, with his silhouette etched in superb likeness, along with words. "Olympic Champion." At the base of the stone, water flowed over crystal, a symbol of Ekaterina's eternal tears of sadness. I couldn't help but remember the look in the pair's eyes, captured on world-wide television.

That look is love. That look is what I feel for my family. That look is what I feel for my daughter, Alexandria Rose.

Jonathan touched my shoulder. I'd been standing, staring, thinking, longer than I realized.

"Ready?"

"Yes."

We had to get back to the hotel, to meet with the doctor for Allie's visa exam.

The exam was short and sweet. At 11 months, Allie was the size of a 3 month old. Her eyes followed movement. She reacted to sounds. Her hands tried to grab, and she "almost sits up." And the doctor said that the scar on the side of her ankle is from the IV tube that kept her alive at the time of her premature birth.

She "passed."

And after dinner at the hotel restaurant off the lobby, we fell into bed.

Almost there. Almost there.

Tomorrow: The American Embassy and our flight home.

Thank God.

Chapter Thirty-Three

The Last Leg

On Monday morning, Sergei picked us up from our hotel and drove us to the American Embassy. Dozens of uniformed American soldiers stood guard.

Americans! Speaking English! I wanted to kiss them.

For two hours, we sat in a crowded room with plastic molded chairs and linoleum floor. All around us, all kinds of people – and American families with newly adopted children – sat and squirmed and talked. How refreshing, to speak without a translator. What a relief, to see other adoptive parents.

"Wait. Stand in line. Be patient," said Sergei. "It is no big deal."

And it wasn't. I caught myself talking in broken English to Americans and laughed. Allie sat on my lap and pumped her hands up and down, pulled at my shirt, and slapped at the back of the plastic chair.

"Conner?" The voice boomed from behind the bullet-proof window.

We rose and carried Allie to stand with us and face the gentleman, who, by the way, was all business.

"Did you meet this child before you adopted her?"

"Yes," we answered in unison.

He scribbled on his form.

"Congratulations."

That was it. One word and a brief smile.

A photo. A packet of papers. And we were out the door.

One more step in our journey, the colors of the sunset streaked into the clouds, making lines of beautiful rays of peach and yellow against the azure sky.

We drove to the airport. Time spun faster. The air bounced full of anticipation.

It was time to leave Russia. And I was ready.

Sergei shooed away the beggars zeroing in on us at the airport door by placing a few coins in their open palms. Brisk steps took us to another airline counter. I was getting used to balancing Allie on one hip and balancing my carry bag hanging from my other shoulder.

Amazing, how fast the "baby stuff" comes back. Feels just the same as when Michael and Thomas were little.

And again, we stood at the gate, ready to board the plane.

"Dasveedanya," Sergei said, genuine and professional. A brief goodbye. Fitting, for him. But it wasn't enough for me.

I pulled out my friend, the Journal.

"Sergei – will you write in Alexandria's Journal?"

He smiled. "Of course."

And he wrote:

Dear Alexandria Rose.
You decorated my life last three days. God blesses you my dear girl.
Sergei

I looked at the writing, puzzled.

"Do you know Kenny Rogers, yes?"

"Yes," I said.

"You decorated my life. This is a good song, yes?"

Jonathan and I smiled.

"And your daughter, she is beautiful. Jonathan, I think you will need to keep a baseball bat near the front door when she is older."

We chuckled, grasped hands, and then grabbed our bags to board the plane to Amsterdam.

It was a smooth and uneventful flight. Allie slept. I snuck a catnap. We landed just fine, found our way through the beautiful airport just fine, and though it was dark, found our hotel easily.

I didn't like the fact that there were no flights to America until the next morning. But again, there was nothing we could do about it.

Nothing but feel the joy of being together as a threesome, anticipating our arrival home.

Allie slept in a real crib that night. Jonathan "crashed" into the queen-sized bed and slept soundly. I slipped away into the bathroom and drew a steamy bath with clear, clean water – something I hadn't seen in days.

My emotions flowed out in release. Tears bubbled in happiness and relief for our new daughter. I sobbed for the babies left behind. I cried because I missed my boys. And I cried because I suddenly wanted my mom to hold me, just like when I was a little girl.

I dabbed my body and face with the plush white towel, crawled into comfortable but ready-to-be-washed night clothes, and then slept. Deeply.

Time flew forward. The morning burst on us, bright and noisy. We boarded our flight to America, known as "The Baby Flight" because so many adoptive families booked this particular flight home.

Our flight attendant brought a crib that clipped onto the wall, and for almost the entire flight across the Atlantic, Allie lay on her back and played with her fingers, toes, and small toys we pulled from our bag. She opened and closed her fist. She punched her hand into the air at an unseen playmate. She kept herself busy and didn't seem to need much at all. I watched in wonder.

This must be how she played in the orphanage.

Hours passed. Looking out the window, I saw the land and my heart rushed.

We're on the other side of the ocean!!

I picked up Allie from the crib.

"Look, sweetie!"

She writhed.

"Oh, OK, OK. Here you go." I placed her back in the crib, and she was fine.

As the land changed from dark mottled green to blue-dashed lakes, I decided to feed Allie a bit before landing. But we were out of powdered formula. So I gave her apple juice in the bottle.

She slurped and guzzled frantically in agitated delight. When the last drop passed her lips, Allie fussed. Jonathan waved a toy in Allie's face, catching her eye in distraction. And then the seatbelt light blinked, along with the familiar, "Ding, ding. Ding, ding."

We're landing.

The rest blurred forward.

A clicking chorus of seatbelts. Stuffing things back in the carry on. Feeling the bumps in our stomach and painful ear pops. The jolt of the wheels violently jerking on the touch-down. Hot air and many voices in muffled murmuring. Balancing baby and bag and bumping "excuse-me" before and behind. Breezy air pungent with plane exhaust. Tunnel walking. The gate. Down the hall. And another hall. And into Customs.

Lines. More lines.

Where do we go?

"May I help you?" The stranger-official's voice pulled Jonathan out of the line and into the office. I followed, Allie turning in my arms to look at faces.

"May I see your envelope?" Handing him the fat manila envelope, we shifted our bags, hoping all was well.

He shuffled documents, read, and shuffled again. He marked a mark and stamped a stamp. And then a wave and a smile.

"Congratulations – She's beautiful!"

And now more walking. And walking. And walking. With barely enough time to get to our connecting flight, my forehead sweat and my legs ached. Fatigue set in. Jonathan's face kept forward and his pace stayed determined. My body screamed to rest, but I couldn't.

Almost there. Almost home. I can do this. I can find the energy.

Then the apple juice that we'd given Allie on the plane came back to haunt us. Too strong for her system, we had what I'll call a "diaper explosion."

All I could think was, *not now!*

We ran onto the connecting plane just in time before the door closed. As soon as the plane ascended, I balanced Allie the best I could as to not ruin my clothes and walked back to the bathroom to clean her up.

The smell was horrible, and the destruction on her clothing was worse. While washing Allie head-to-toe with baby wipes and dribbling water from the mini-sink, the overhead announcement rang out: "Please be seated. We'll be starting our descent momentarily."

I don't know how, but I did it; I made her fresh again and popped on a new outfit. Back in my seat, Jonathan leaned over with comic exaggeration and sniffed.

"Much better!"

Then it hit me: In a few short minutes, we'd be all together.

A sigh to beat all sighs left my lips. Jonathan put his hand on my arm.

"We did it," he said. "We're here."

Praise God. I am SO ready to be home.

And the wheels of the plane touched down.

Chapter Thirty-Four

Home

I saw Mom first. Her face glowed. Her eyes glittered with tears. Michael and Thomas stood on either side of Mom. I saw the boy's faces, then the pink Mylar balloons rising from sticks held tight in their fists, with the words, "It's a girl!"

And there is Sarah. And Molly and Rob and Katie. And...Oh, my boys in my arms feel so delicious! Everyone around....Jonathan? Jonathan? There you are!

Together....All of us! We're together!

Kisses, hugs – boy squeezes and camcorders held from extended arms above the crowd. Smiles and laughter and spilling of words together. Michael touching Allie's forehead, Thomas' gentle touches on Allie's arm. Jonathan wrapping his arms around the boys, making bear-hug noises. Allie's smiles. Picture flashes and blinks. The woman next to us – a stranger – pulled into the rush of our beautiful moment, crying with us in joy.

Joy. Yes, giggly, indescribable joy.

Waters of joy held me buoyant in the fatigue. My mind floated above the swirling happiness of all of us here, together.

I remembered the moment when we began our adoption journey. I think I called it "the moment of true dark meeting the first sliver of arriving dawn."

The sun was now setting beautiful goldens and bright oranges and fiery reds – a glorious moment of a "day" well spent.

I felt above, looking down and back on the entire experience, with my eyes wide open, now. The path, much longer and harder than I'd thought, traveled into the horizon behind me, its features distinct and pressed strong into my memory. Strong into my heart. Strong into my soul.

I am forever changed by this experience. And it is good. It is a good change.

Funny thing, though. I thought the path of our adoption journey was the event to conquer, the occasion to prevail through, the mountain to climb.

But I'm at the top of the mountain. And guess what? I see a wide and broad view. It's a view of rows and rows of mountain ranges in front of me. A whole new land to traverse.

I think I'll need another Journal.

My story with Alexandria Rose is only just beginning.

Postscript from Erin

Would you like to know more? Read the following pages. They're full of "ways to help" and "good things to do" – Your specific words of encouragement as waiting moms and dads, grandparents, friends, and children who are adopted.

Find your "section" and learn a little bit more about how you can fully enjoy the adoption process. And if you have further questions, feel free to email me at Erin@ErinBrownConroy.com. If you have questions for Elle, send them along, too. Because of the next two books' content, and in order to protect Elle's family, Elle will continue to maintain anonymity. But I'll make sure your emails get to her.

You might be wondering, "What happens next? What's the rest of Elle and Allie's story?" Keep on the lookout for Book Two in the series, *The Other Side of Broken*, and Book Three, *Daughter of my Heart*. Let me just say, the first months home are unique, wonderful, and challenging. And yes, sometimes devastating. The story continues. Visit the web site, www.ParentingYourAdoptedChild.com to find out more.

Thank you for traveling with us, entering into our story, and sharing these moments together. We look forward to connecting with you again soon.

Warm regards,
Erin

For Waiting Moms and Dads Only

To say that the journey to your child is an extraordinary, beautiful journey – one that changes your life forever – is stating the obvious, isn't it? You know in your heart and soul how this path is exciting and, in many ways, terrifying, too. As one who has traveled the path many times, may I share some thoughts to make the path brighter – and easier? Because I know that knowledge brings comfort, assurance, and strength to our journey – and as adoptive parents, we can use comfort, assurance, and strength.

The Beginning. The beginning of the process can feel unnerving. For any adoption, we, as Elle in her story, "peer this way and that, trying to distinguish features and distinctiveness to paths, imagining the feeling of our feet pressing into the ground if we chose that particular way."

Adoptions are full of imagining. Some imagining is wonderful – and some is unnerving. We don't know so much of what's ahead. Not knowing is not fun. If you're the kind of person who likes to know what's going to happen, when it will happen, and how it will happen (like me), then the whole process can drive you a bit nutty. Unless you prepare for it.

Right from the start, keep a long-view to the horizon. Expect lack of clarity, delays, and lots of waiting. Seek answers and don't let your thoughts and anticipation turn into stress. Tell yourself truths that move you forward like, "We *will* find answers" and "The journey *will* end – we'll have our child here with us soon." The "long view" keeps us sane and positive, and we enjoy the journey a whole lot more.

The Agency. Choose your agency wisely; you're going to go through a lot together. Think of it as a marriage; yes, you'll be that "involved." Everything you do will be filtered through the values of your agency, so make sure your values line up. More than anything else, you'll need the ability to communicate. So feeling comfortable and "on the same page" is highly important.

What if you've already begun the process and you're facing a struggle with your agency? Then I encourage you to do all you can to communicate well and get answers that help you both feel comfortable. Take the first step to "make it right." If struggles continue, keep in mind that this relationship is significant, but not super-long-term. You'll have post-adoption check-ups and reports to walk through together, but when that's complete, you're a family with no one looking over your shoulder. Do all you can to help your agency do its job, and then your steps together are independent and free.

The Process. Get as much information about your particular adoption process. Because just like they say, information is power. Power to make the right choices. Power to know when to "push for answers" (nicely, of course) and when to wait. Power to spend your time wisely. Power not to worry.

And by all means, enjoy the process. Yes, you can enjoy the wait! When it came to using my physical and emotional time constructively and enjoyably, it took me four adoptions to truly "get it." Like Elle, I yearned and longed and stressed and worried – sometimes a bit much. Now, some of that is normal (just like when pregnant, looking at your big belly, and saying, "Man-oh-man, I can't wait to have you in my arms!"). However, anxiety doesn't have to rule us.

What we say in our minds is extremely important when it comes to whether or not we enjoy the process of adopting our child. Let the good thoughts roll around; breathe in the truth of each moment and savor its essence. Before you know it, your child will be here.

The Organization. Keep papers and processes in order and in a clearly-trackable system – it's a *tremendous* help, saving you from extra stress. Don't underestimate the power of checklists, folders, phone message pads, page protectors, and binders for important documents. In a running log, write down who you talked to, on what day, at what time, and at what phone number. You never know when you'll have to back-track for good information. And for tax purposes, keep receipts in a special folder from the get-go.

Remember, each paper is a hoop to jump through, and every hoop brings you closer to your child. Keep the hoops in a neat little row, and the jumping is easier.

The Adoptive Community. No matter where our child is born, what our child's age, or where we live in this world, all parents adopting share similar steps on the path to our child. Along with the ability to share valuable information together, there's a wonderful dynamic with adoptive parents – an emotional energy of, "Yeah, I know – me too" and "everything is going to work out in the end."

Like Elle's relationship with Molly, I encourage you to find at least one adoptive family who can come alongside you and stand with you through the process. Read magazines and articles, "talk" on message boards, go to adoptive family events, and meet one-on-one with parents with children who are adopted. You'll be richer for it. And it takes a whole lot of stress out of the process.

The Problems. Problems will come. I don't know of one adoption process that "went perfectly." Be mentally and emotionally prepared. You are strong, you are capable, and you are able to find answers to any question or issue that arises. Rest in that knowledge.

Delays will come. Courts and legal systems are notorious for delays – it's the nature of the beast. Keep plugging away. Be confident: The judge will sign. And you'll be ready with the party poppers and champagne when he or she does.

What if it doesn't happen? What if – for whatever reason – the adoption doesn't go through? Yes, that happens. And it's the most devastating feeling. Life stops. The pain is as real as if you held that child in your arms and then the child was whisked away. It's awful.

We have eight children who came to us through adoption. Twice I've had bags packed, ready to travel, and things went awry. The first time, the medical staff "had a hunch" about the baby and, just before putting our child-to-be on a flight, decided to give her an MRI. The results showed severe brain damage, and we had to make the awful decision to say "no" because we didn't feel capable of parenting her. The second time things "went wrong," we were packed to go see our six-month-old. We had fully-translated dossier in hand and all fees paid.

In fact, the entire process had zoomed by, smooth and clear. The day before our flight, we got the phone call: just one hour earlier, our baby had died of illness – an illness that, in the US, is preventable.

Those are extremes; they probably won't happen to you. But they could. A birth mom can change her mind. A family member can come into the picture and claim the child (that happened to us). A child's adoptable status can be "taken back" by the overseas agency and determined "not adoptable" (that happened to us, too).

I don't mean to be negative, but a healthy dose of reality wrapped up in wisdom is good for us to maintain. Keep hope alive. Live in positive expectancy. But if something goes wrong, know that you will be all right. And there is another child who waits for you to be mommy and daddy.

The Memory Makers. I can't stress this enough: It's so important to keep track of the process in some way – either in a journal like Elle or with oodles of videos, still pictures, scrapbooks, and boxes of trinkets and memory-makers. Because when your child is older, these "pieces of history" help your child to mentally and emotionally fill in the picture. Your child's story is invaluable, meaningful, and full of details. Document it all – and then some. Like I've always said – you can't take enough pictures.

Document little details of "the every day" – the car you drove in, the food you ate, the people you met, and so on. Take notes. Yes, save things like the candy wrapper from the international airport and the napkin from the hotel. When your child is older, you can tell her story with flourish and detail. And every detail matters.

Your adoption journey is unique. It's special. It's a brilliant moment in your family's history. Cherish the journey. And, like Elle, when you're at the end of the path, you'll enjoy your "sunset of beautiful goldens and bright oranges and fiery reds – a glorious moment of a 'day' well spent."

For Grandparents Only

Your adult child is going through a wonderful event – a "birth" into the family. Yes, it's true this newly-adopted child isn't joining the family through a literal, physical birth. But your new grandchild is "birthed" into the family just the same.

The adoption process – those months of waiting and working through the in-and-outs, the ups-and-downs, with the questions and concerns – it's so very much like a pregnancy. And just like in Elle's story, the moment of meeting an adopted child is beautiful and brilliant – shining with absolute joy. It is the amazing moment of a child joining the family with the exact value and benefits as a birth child.

May I share with you some thoughts to help you become closer to your adult child and your new grandchild? Because I know that your involvement – and your thoughts, feelings, and actions – are invaluable and precious to the entire family.

The Beginning. The whole idea of adoption might be a new one to you. Let me assure you, adopting is a wonderful journey – one that you're an intricate part of. It's also something your adult child isn't entering into lightly. He or she has thought deeply about adopting a new son or daughter – and have come to the decision that for his or her family, this is the absolute best step to take. Inside your adult child's heart, there's a deep desire to share love with a child who has no mother or father. That desire is unexplainable but incredibly real. Your acceptance and support are gifts to give.

Are you wondering how it all works? Your kind questions are welcomed. Are you wondering if your adult child can afford the cost of an adoption? Don't worry – these are things your adult child has thought through, for many long hours. Are you worried that the child may be "different"? Well, most assuredly, an internationally-adopted child may be different – especially in skin color, eye shape, and hair texture. And body shape, height and weight. And in activity level. And in learning style. And oh, there are so many ways your new grandchild can be different (Remember, you can have two children from the same birth parent, and they can be incredibly different too!). Those differences aren't negative; they're positive. They're special. They add richness and beauty to your family tree.

And in many ways, your adopted grandchild will also be *the same*. He or she will learn to smile, walk, and talk in the same manner as the rest of the family. She may learn to giggle like her mom and he may learn to move his arm to cast the fishing rod just like dad; she may become a beautiful seamstress like grandma and he might learn to love woodworking like grandpa. Your new grandchild will blend into your family well – and you have a huge part in it all.

Take this opportunity to learn, grow, and become closer as a family through the process – with your acceptance and encouragement to be him- or herself, whether different or the same.

The Process. It's a long process, this adoption thing. It takes a lot of physical and emotional energy. It's good energy – but energy nonetheless. What does all this energy-spending have to do with you? Everything!

Can you help through the process? Absolutely. Think "pregnancy." How would you help in a pregnancy? Like Elle's mother, would you stay with the children during the trip? Like her father-in-law, would you make a bunk bed? Would you help paint the new child's bedroom? Would you help put together a memory book? Would you help pick out clothes or a stroller or a toddler's bike or a pre-teen's toys or…? Well, you get the idea. Whatever you'd do for a birth grandchild, do the same for your newly-adopted grandchild. This is a role only you can play. And no matter the age of your adopted grandchild, your role is highly-esteemed, highly-valued, and highly-needed.

The Problems. If your adult child had a problem with a pregnancy, what would you do then? My guess is that you'd do everything possible to support your adult child. When problems and struggles come in the adoption process, I encourage you to "be there" for your adult child. With words of support and gracious actions, distinctively stand as the pillar that sustains, the boat that buoys up, and the bar that helps bear weight. You, like no one else on this earth, are in the exclusive position to bless your adult child in word, thought, and deed.

Your Position. How special it is, to have a grandparent! Your grandchild is gaining a whole family, with all of the branches to hold him or her up. Oh, how glorious it is, to have a strong family tree! Will you be a part of that strength?

If your adult child is becoming a parent for the first time, he or she may struggle a bit – but we both know that's normal. Be gracious and gentle in your approach to the challenges of having a child. If your newly-adopted grandchild is a second, third, fifth, or tenth child, then your adult child may just need your physical support. Ask if there's any way you can help.

And if your newly-adopted grandchild is an older child, you can bet that he or she knows how important it is to have grandparents who are involved and loving. Our son who was adopted at age eight was incredibly excited to have grandparents. From the get-go, he asked, "When can I see them? Will they like me? Can I spend time with them?" In his orphanage, some boys' and girls' grandparents visited children. The other children oohed and aahed and envied those with grandparents. On top of that, his original Eastern-European culture honors the position of grandparent in a reverence-type of honor. That all added up to an "I-can't-wait-to-have-grandparents!" longing.

It's a longing for relationship. For value. For being cherished – by mom, dad, brother, sister, uncle, aunt, cousin, and grandparent. Grandparents, give what you can to support, encourage, and stand by your adult child. Let your adult child be the parent. Respect their boundaries. Be available and involved in healthy interaction. Then, within those healthy boundaries, open up your heart and wrap your arms around your newly-adopted grandchild in acceptance. That love will come full circle back to you, completing the family and giving your new grandchild his or her precious place in the world.

And isn't that what it's all about?

For Friends of Adoptive Families

Your friend is "pregnant"! Yes, the adoption process is much like pregnancy, isn't it? As you see from Elle's story, it's a time of terribly-tough waiting, sometimes-bothersome worrying, and overall-hopeful wondering about the future. May I share with you some thoughts that will allow you to be a better friend? Because your support, encouragement, and help are invaluable – and as a friend, isn't that what we want to be? So please – step with me through the issues of the adoption's "pregnancy" – and be a great friend.

The Process. As you know from reading this book, the adoption process is full of frustrating unknowns, unanswered questions, and seemingly-endless waiting. As a friend, your special role through the process is one of encouragement and support. But how can you encourage and support when you don't know very much about the whole thing? How can you help in the middle of so many frustrations, unanswered questions, and long periods of waiting?

It's simple. Just ask.

"What can I do for you? How can I help? Is there anything that I can do for your family right now?" These questions are warm, open-ended conversation starters guaranteed to help your friend. When you're open, available, and full of sensitive questions, you're being the best friend that you can be.

The Terminology. In adoption, there are specific "politically-correct" terms to use. But it's not just about being politically-correct. It's about the way we view the child. And it's about the way we accept the child – with the same rights, privileges, and intrinsic value – as a complete member of the family. Here are "the basics."

"Real child." In speaking about kids, don't talk about the "real child" and the "adopted child." The adopted child *is* a real child.

"Adopted child." Don't differentiate between siblings. There is no difference. Our child is our child. Not a step child. Not a birth child.

Not an adopted child. Just a child. We're a family together, and no lines need to be drawn.

"Real parents." The adoptive parents *are* the real parents. Real parents care for the child day-in-and-day-out, sit at the sick child's bed, and perform the daily tasks of being mom and dad. The "birth parent" or "biological parent" is the person who biologically gave birth to the child.

Privacy. Sometimes people ask families in the process of adoption (or who have their child home) some pretty invasive questions – and make some pretty outrageous statements. You don't have to be in that group. You're going to be knowledgeable and sensitive.

Here are some helpful hints for respect and privacy.

1. Don't ask about the child's birth family, foster family, or orphanage situation. This information is private. There may be issues or sensitivities that aren't appropriate to be shared. It's okay for you not to know. If your friend offers the information, that's fine. Just don't go fishing for it – because you want to be respectful.
2. Don't talk about the child as if he or she is an object. I know this sounds funny, but let me tell you, there are many times when families feel as if others consider their child a "cute pet" or "sweet thing" to pat on the head. Just because the child looks different from the rest of the family doesn't mean we jibber and jabber silly words and oooh and aaah as if looking at an imported vase. Be sensitive to saying words and acting toward the child in realistic, rational, normal ways – the same ways you'd act toward another child in the family.
3. Don't talk about the child in front of the child. Even if the child is a baby, it's important to keep comments general and out of the "private" realm. What is private? Anything that is talking about what the child says, does, acts like, and looks like. Family and individuals' privacy is a good practice for *all* children. It's just not healthy to talk about a child in front of the child.

4. Be careful to keep personal space boundaries. We all have a "personal bubble" of appropriate space between us. When the new child arrives, be sensitive to not touch the child's face or body, stand or sit in the child's personal space, or reach out to touch or pick up the child. It's invasive. Also, children who are adopted often have to learn about boundaries; your appropriate respect of boundaries helps them to learn. And lastly, some children have what are called "attachment issues." That means the child doesn't have an appropriate sense of attachment to primary family, including mom and dad. The child may "go to anyone" – jumping in the arms of complete strangers. While it seems wonderful that your friend's child is "treating you so warmly," it really isn't wonderful. It's not healthy. Emotionally healthy children *don't* give hugs and kisses freely; they save "special expressions" for family. Help your friend teach the child healthy behavior by not encouraging overly-touchy actions to those outside the immediate family.

Asking questions. We're all curious. Sometimes it's appropriate to ask questions, and sometimes it's not. When it comes to questions, you and your friend have to be on the same page. The best thing to do is to *ask* your friend if he or she would *tell you* when a question is "out of bounds" – and to tell you in kindness. Here are some guidelines for questions:
1. As in Elle's story, sometimes we just want to support our friend with a, "How are you? How's it going?" question....And we don't realize that we're the bazillionth person to ask that particular question. Perhaps the thing to do is to ask, "Is this a good time to ask about how things are going?" or "I want to show you that I care. Right now, how can I do that best?" My guess is that your friend will freely tell you what is best. And you'll both feel comfortable.
2. Try not to ask questions of the siblings. One of my birth daughters says that when she was younger, she felt

"trapped" by adults (especially those she didn't know very well) asking invasive questions like, "Do you like having siblings who are adopted?" and "What's it like to have a brother or sister who is adopted?" and ""So – What was it like, when your little brother came on the plane?" To her, it's like asking, "So, what was your mother's birthing experience? How long was the labor? Do you like having siblings who are birthed to your mom?" Pretty silly, in her mind. And pretty uncomfortable. Just be careful.
3. Try to ask deeper questions at appropriate times, like when the two of you are alone, having a cup of tea – and not when you're in line at the grocery store. And again, if the "signals" from your friend are, "I'd rather not talk about it," then respect her signals.

Being a Friend. While your friend waits for the child to arrive home, offer emotional support by saying encouraging and uplifting words. Be a great listener: nod, smile, and empathetically say "mmhmm" in positive-ness, showing your friend that you're "engaged." You may not understand all your friend is struggling with. That's okay. Your listening speaks volumes. Offer physical support by helping out around the house, watching the other children, and cooking a meal. You know your friend best. Do what you know. Let this experience be one that binds you together and, when in doubt – ask. Your friend will appreciate your concern, honesty, and sensitivity.

For Children who are Adopted

As you've read Elle's story, my guess is that you've experienced many thoughts and feelings. May I share some ideas with you that will help open doors of even deeper understanding? Because I know that understanding can do three things.

Understanding can create a greater peace with who you are in your place in this world. It can take you to a place where you can share your beauty and strength with others. And it can help you enjoy each moment of your life, knowing what a precious gift you are to your parents, to your extended family, and to your friends.

Your Story. In reading Elle's story, I'm sure you couldn't have helped but revisit your own story. Do you wonder about the intricate details of how you came to be in your family? Maybe this is the time to ask your parents about the details, particulars, and the fine points of your own story.

For Elle, did you notice how precious and special each moment was in the journey? Did you catch the love in Elle's journaling? I venture to say, you couldn't miss it. Have you ever realized how much you were wanted? Desired? Longed for? Wonder no more.

Did you ever realize how waiting for the adoption is similar to waiting for a biological birth? Time passing slowly, the preparing, the arrival, the pictures – though different, it's somehow the same. Ask you adoptive mom and dad about their experience. I bet you'll find poignant, silly, and meaningful memories that add details and depth to your story. Because your story is something to talk about and enjoy with others (especially with your own children, some day).

Your Parents. Elle's story helps put into perspective what your parents went through to get to you. Perhaps reading these words solidified your understanding of how much your parents love you. It took a lot of effort, commitment, and hard work to bring you home. Yes, you're that special.

What that "work" does is strengthen your parents' resolve to give you the absolute best that they can give. Over the last 20 years, I've met hundreds of adoptive parents, and it's always the same: commitment, involvement, care to keep their child safe, and strong love in actions and words. After all, we worked so hard to get to you – we're going to give our absolute best effort to keep you healthy and strong, and to give you everything else good under the sun!

Seriously, it may feel like your parents are "going overboard" sometimes. Don't worry – they aren't. They just appreciate who you are. And they're thankful that they have you.

Do you sometimes wonder if your adoptive parents are your "real" parents? Let me tell you, they absolutely are.

Lara, my oldest daughter who is adopted and now an adult, says: "You are my parents – you always have been and always will be. The older I get, the more I realize that everything works together. You were called to be my mother; I was called to be your child. Second Chronicles 16:9 says, 'For the eyes of the Lord run to and fro throughout the whole earth, to show Himself strong on behalf of those whose heart is loyal to Him.' Our moms and dads traveled 'throughout the earth' to get to us, and because of a parent's love, God shows Himself strong in my life and yours."

Your Future. Be proud of your story. You are unique, special, and loved. It doesn't matter whether you joined your family by birth or by adoption – you are an intricate and priceless part of your family.

Jeremiah 29 verse 11 says, "For I know the thoughts I have toward you, says the Lord. Thoughts of peace and not of evil, to give you a future and a hope." Your future is bright and full of hope. God's plan includes the past, present, and future. He designed – and continues to design – your life. So rest in who you are – and enjoy your journey ahead.

About the Authors

Elle Conner is a mom of three children - two birth sons and a daughter adopted as an infant from Russia. Elle lives in Michigan, where she works part-time and enjoys raising her children. Though this is the true story of the family's adoption, "Elle Conner" is not her real name. *Miracle in the City of Angels* is the first of three books chronicling their family's experience with two adoptions: Book One – this book – is their infant daughter's adoption story; Book Two follows the joys and challenges of raising a child from an orphanage with multiple sensory challenges; and Book Three follows the heartbreak of a second adoption of an older child that disrupted. The books, filled with pleasure and pain, are raw and personal accounts from Elle's private journals.

Erin Brown Conroy, MA, is a mom of 13 children – three by birth, two through marriage, and eight through international adoption. She is the author of the books, *20 Secrets to Success with Your Child* (2003), *My Kid is Driving Me Crazy! 14 Realistic Expectations that Make Parenting Easier* (2004), *40 Days to Balanced Parenting* (2004), and the *Totally Fit Mom "Life at its Best!" program* (2005). Featured in national media such as *Parents* and *Parenting* magazines, *The Chicago Tribune, Dallas Morning News,* and *Miami Herald,* and on numerous national radio shows, she hosts web sites and writes a national column on parenting. Erin teaches as adjunct faculty for Cornerstone University in writing, leadership, research, management, and health and wellness. She and her husband enjoy living in Michigan and home schooling nine of their ten children still living at home.